Enough

Falling for a Rose Book Two

By

Stephanie Nicole Norris

Enough

Falling for a Rose Book Two

Dedication

To my reading family, thank you for your continuous support!

Chapter One

Claudia Stevens rose to her feet and tapped the sterling silverware against the champagne flute. "Can I have everyone's attention please?"

In a room filled with curious stares and elated smiles, Claudia gathered the courage to speak from her heart. She turned slightly to her right and offered a grin to her best friend and business partner, Samiyah Manhattan and her dazzling groom, Jonas Alexander Rose.

"I'd like to make a toast to the bride and groom."

Hands holding champagne flutes went up in the air.

"Samiyah, you deserve everything life has to offer you especially the man of your dreams." Samiyah's beam grew across her face. "With him, I do believe you two will have your happily ever after and most likely a football field of children."

Snickers went throughout the room, and someone said, "You can say that again!" More laughter trickled about as everyone turned to Christopher Lee Rose, father of the groom.

"I love you girl; may the joys of your heart remain everlasting."

"Here! Here!" Someone yelled.

"I'm not done," Claudia said lifting a finger. More snickers. "To my new best friend, Jonas, thank you for showing my girl what true love is. Continue that tradition... or I'm coming for you." More laughter danced about, and Claudia was happy for the interruption. It gave her time to concentrate her next words to the happy couple without focusing on the ripple of heat that flowed across the room in waves. Claudia shifted her weight; her short bob style hair swaying just below her ears. With controlled purpose, Claudia coached herself into not meeting the gaze of the six-foot two-inch specimen that had haunted her dreams every night for the last six months. Feeling ruffled, Claudia took her fingers through her straight mane and quickly down her neck.

"You have nothing to fear," Jonas replied to her as more snickers sounded throughout the room.

"I'm just checking," Claudia responded. "I wish you both prosperity, peace, and love in all of your endeavors. Congratulations! You two are truly meant for each other."

Glasses clinked, and everyone sipped their champagne. Unable to help herself, Claudia stole a glance in his direction and was caught up in the undertow of his dark stare. Her belly flipped, and she watched as his tongue snaked out of his mouth and slid across his divine lips. Heat suffused her cheeks, neck, and breasts causing her nipples to grow hard instantaneously. His gaze was unwavering and potent; making no mistake of his intentions to seduce her from across the expensively decorated room.

Enough

Claudia lifted the flute to her lips and took down the rest of the sweet bubbly liquid. She turned and fled her seat making sure to grab another flute off the tray of a nearby server on her way outside the extravagant tent that had been set up for the wedding party. Stepping into the sand, Claudia reached down, quickly removing the five-inch Christian Louboutins that adorned her feet.

The mild wind that ran across her shoulders was a sweet relief on the warmth of her skin. He always did that to her. Jaden Alexander Rose had been a distraction ever since she'd met him. Of course, upon meeting Jaden months ago, Claudia welcomed that interference. She was over the same type of men. The ones that pretended to be interested but just wanted sexual favors. The men who were attentive but had a wife and kids at home. The kind who simply didn't know how to treat a woman right. Her life had been riddled with those types and Claudia longed for someone to call her own and vice versa. However, that someone hadn't come along until she met Jaden Alexander Rose.

They were both attending the March of Dimes gala event, and Claudia was being auctioned off for a date in exchange for a hefty donation. She wasn't alone. Samiyah, and their co-workers Selena Strauss and Octavia Davenport were also a part of the event when seven of the sexiest men, elite in stature, strolled in their direction. Claudia had almost choked on her alcoholic beverage. When the seven gentleman surrounded her and Samiyah, Claudia's eyes never left Jaden. As ridiculously gorgeous as the men were, Jaden stuck out

3

like a sore thumb with his broad shoulders, golden brown eyes, goatee and fresh white smile. His hair was cut and cropped to the shape of his face. Samiyah introduced her to Jonas and Jonas in return introduced Claudia to his brothers. Claudia's hearing had eluded her after he said Jaden's name. Besides being his brother, Jaden was also Jonas's business partner at Rose Bank and Trust Credit Union.

Jaden, being at the top of his game, was named on Forbes 30 under 30 finance list as one of the youngest traders, bankers, and dealmakers. Currently running his own $730 million-dollar hedge fund at Rose Bank and Trust Credit Union, Jaden traded oil after the devastation of hurricane Gustav and Ike. His accolades didn't end there. The list went on and on, and Jaden continued to be one of Chicago's most notorious movers and shakers.

With Jaden being so influential and always turning heads whenever he was around, Claudia only mused over a possible relationship with him in her own head. She would never elude to this out loud because the possibility of a man like Jaden being with an 'around the way girl' like Claudia seemed unrealistic if spoken.

Claudia grew up in the hood of Chicago, attended public schools and took out financial aid for college tuition. Her father disappeared when she was twelve-years-old, leaving her mother, Adeline Stevens to raise Claudia and her older sister, Desiree. Their household was as unstable as Hurricane Ike. Claudia quickly got into trouble after her father's departure; skipping classes to smoke marijuana behind the stands by the racetrack.

Claudia and Desiree were two peas in a pod until Claudia's behavior became reckless, landing them both in juvenile for forgery. Claudia had asked Desiree to sign their mother's signature on what was supposed to be a Jr High school progress report. But in turn, it was an application for a small loan at a local mom and pops bank. The incident caused a rift in the sister's relationship, and Desiree had been skeptical of Claudia's motives since then. Never mind that the incident occurred over a decade ago. Since that time, Claudia provided everything their mother required over the last five years since she needed full-time care after her stroke.

Claudia's toes sank into the brown grains of sand as she placed one foot in front of the other with her shoes clutched in her palms. Claudia and Jaden had flirted countless times and had intense and sensual conversations. She'd even met his father, brothers, and sisters, but that seemed to be the gist of it. Where it appeared they were easily connected, Jaden had taken multiple business trips without as much as a phone call. And in Claudia's mind, Jaden had more important things to do and could have any woman at his disposal. For this reason, she rationalized that the chemistry between she and Jaden was all primal and silly thoughts of being in love with him was absurd.

So unfortunately for Claudia, she would have to keep an eye out for her mister right no matter how bad she didn't want to look past Jaden.

A soft wind fell over her, and Claudia's hair lifted in its current. She stopped walking to take in the sights of the midnight waves rushing the shoreline. The cool water crowded her feet; washing up to her ankles. Claudia threw her arms around herself and closed her eyes, inhaling the ocean's natural sea salt scent.

"If this was your attempt to hide from me, you're not doing a very good job at it."

A rush of warmth covered Claudia. Chills caused the fine hair on her mocha chocolate skin to rise. Her dark brown eyes opened, and her breath was caught in her throat. Trying with desperation to regain her sense of control, Claudia couldn't help but be taken by the dark beat in his tone.

She turned slowly; the wind pulling her tresses away from her slanted eyes. "Why would I need to hide from you?" Claudia's eyebrows rose.

"The jury is still out on that, but I'm going to find out. So, tell me, Claudia," her name sounded like silk on his tongue, "what brings you out to the shore alone after giving such a humorous toast?"

Claudia smirked. "Humorous? You find me funny, Mr. Rose?"

Jaden tisked, "Now you're deflecting." Claudia blushed but kept her comments to herself.

"You didn't think I'd notice," he asked.

"I'm not. I just asked a question. But since you're bent on my answering yours, I'll be honest with you," Claudia said. "I needed to get some fresh air. This seemed to be the best place for it."

A mischievous smiled scurried across his features, and Jaden took in a deep breath, moving a step closer to her. "Is that all?"

His voice rumbled, and now her skin felt like scales as the chills deepened on her flesh. Claudia's hands absentmindedly rubbed her shoulders.

Mistaking her shivers for coolness, Jaden removed the expensive casual shirt he'd changed into after the ceremony and covered her so quickly Claudia didn't have a chance to refuse him. The masculine scent of his body glazed her in a layer of perpetual allure.

Jaden moved to cover her further with his strong arms embracing her snugly; her face now resting against his bare chest. Claudia's breathing became abnormal. At least to her. Being in such close proximity to Jaden was causing her body to run haywire; every nerve, ready and able to jump off a cliff. It wasn't beneath Claudia to turn her nose into the crook of his neck, so she did; resting her lips against his bobbing apple.

Although they'd had many conversations in the past, this is the closest the two had physically come in contact with each other. For heaven's sake, Claudia wasn't aloof to his seductive charm, but she'd kept her distance in hopes that she wouldn't make a fool of herself when her body betrayed her and pounced on him. Yet, here he was with his arms around her, cuddling her so close that if he decided to take her here and now she would give herself up to him.

As if he'd read her thoughts, Jaden pulled back, his face hovering above hers. His eyes roamed across her appearance, taken in slanted eyes, full pouty lips, tipped nose and soft smooth skin. Claudia held her breath even though she didn't think herself worthy of him; she would let this moment linger and go wherever he wanted it to.

"You have the most beautiful eyes Claudia, and I've spent many nights dreaming of your lips." Inch by inch he moved his face closer to hers. "It's been hell trying to be a gentleman around you."

"Why?"

"There's this thing that happens when we inhabit the same space. I'd like to hope that you're aware since you tend to disappear soon after."

Claudia was stuck in his gaze, dark and penetrating; his lips mere inches from hers. So what was she waiting on? Why hadn't she lunged like she'd imagined herself doing so many times before? Suddenly, Claudia moved; but it wasn't the foreseen movement she'd imagined it to be. Slowly, she wiggled out of his embrace, her eyes downcast. She took a hand over the back of her neck then cranked her face up to meet his questionable stare.

"Did I say something wrong?"

There was a moment of silence. "No, of course not." She reached to squeeze her neck again then smoothed her hands down his shirt to her waist. Jaden reached out lifting her chin with his finger.

"Tell me what's wrong."

The silence grew around them again. Jaden took a step towards her, and Claudia took a step back.

Jaden lifted his hands in surrender. "I don't mean any harm, baby girl."

Claudia turned her back to him and rolled her eyes. She was being ridiculous, all because her insecurities were hitting her hard. Claudia had no business being with a man like Jaden Rose even if they were based solely on carnal feelings. Claudia felt him move closer, now standing to the side of her back.

"Would it help if I kept my hands to myself," he asked.

No, Claudia thought. *It would be better if you'd have your way with me.* A smile tugged at her lips. "You're fine," she said finally. "I'm all inside my head. I think this wedding is doing something to me."

"I'm glad I'm not the only one."

Claudia's smile grew.

"Would I be intruding to ask you about those thoughts?" Jaden proposed.

"Yes, you would be."

"I hope you don't mind too much if I ask anyway."

Quiet laughter left her. "Very funny, Mr. Rose." Claudia ran an eye over the length of him. "Why do you care what my thoughts are?"

"I don't know," Jaden considered. "Must be that thing I spoke of earlier. When I'm around you, I want to know everything."

"What about when you're not around me?"

Jaden reached out to cup her chin. His thumb circled her lips, his eyes blazing into hers.

Laughter from afar pulled Claudia's attention. The wedding party was on full blast, and it was an opportune time for Claudia to flee. She grabbed for his hand pulling

9

it from her face, their fingers threaded and Jaden squeezed.

"Maybe we should get back to the party. You are the best man and I the maid of honor; we should be in attendance."

"The wedding is over; no one needs us."

"You can't be sure of that," Claudia responded.

She side stepped him. Before walking away, she removed his shirt and handed it back to him managing to get another glimpse of his washboard abs and broad shoulders before completely sauntering off. Her steps had taken her three strides when he called out.

"Claudia."

Her footsteps slowed, and she cast a glance over her shoulder.

"You can run, but you can't hide."

Chapter Two

When Claudia stepped back into the wedding party, she immediately made a beeline for the ladies' room. "Excuse me," she said moving through the swinging door past a woman leaving.

With her heels back on her feet, Claudia strolled to the sink and turned on the faucet; holding her hands under the downpour of warm water. A heavy sigh escaped her. What was going on with her? Claudia didn't think of herself as timid. Nor did she ever feel embarrassed by her past. However, being around Jaden made all her flaws rise to the surface, and she didn't like it one bit.

Claudia was just fine with being her spunky, flirtatious, humorous self, and as much as she adored Jaden from afar, being so close left Claudia feeling unsuitable.

"Get it together," she scolded at her reflection. "If a man can't accept you with your past then forget him."

Even as she gave herself a pep talk, Claudia's mind struggled with the words.

"Ugh!" Claudia turned on her heels and left the bathroom. Back in the main tent, Samiyah was dancing with Jonas. She'd changed from the wedding gown previously worn into the body fitting knee length bandage dress and white Christian Louboutins taking her look to a whole new level of sexy. Claudia smiled, sincerely happy for her girl. Lord knows Samiyah had been through tough times when her ex-husband revealed he'd been cheating and wanted a divorce.

It was all Claudia could do to keep Samiyah from killing him when she'd first found out, but those days were long past her. And that ex-husband of hers could eat her heart out.

Claudia's vision scurried across the room, landing on bridesmaids, which consisted of Jonas' three sisters; Eden, Phoebe, and Jasmine Alexandria Rose. They were dancing with Derek James Clark, Luke Steele, and Quentin Davidson. The three men were fraternity brothers of Jonathon and Jacob and just as drop dead gorgeous.

It should be a sin and a shame to have so much deliciousness in one room, Claudia thought. With her mind back in a healthy place, Claudia sauntered to the dessert table and grabbed a small bowl of grapes. Moving to the next table, she helped herself to another flute of champagne. Claudia continued to peruse the wedding party. The excitement in the building was hard to resist. Suddenly she felt calmer, her spirits lifted.

"Hey, young lady."

Claudia turned to Christopher Lee Rose, Jaden's father. Christopher was a replica of all his sons combined. Despite his fifty-five years, at first glance, one would think Christopher was also a Rose brother. His height at 6'6 made him a giant over Claudia, and his weight was easily 275 pounds. Broad shoulders and a toned build weren't dismissed in his suit and jacket. But most of all, Claudia loved his slick hair that sat in a short crop to his head. Christopher held his hand out. "May I have this dance?"

The smile extended on her lips, and she put the bowl and champagne flute down on the table. "I would love that," she said.

Christopher led her to the dance floor, and they moved to the beat of the jazz band playing.

"Are you enjoying yourself?" Christopher inquired.

Claudia gave a short nod. "I am."

"Good, I enjoyed your toast."

Claudia giggled. "Thanks, I was serious, but everyone seems to think my words held a bit of humor."

They moved in circles around each other. "I believe you know it did."

Claudia shrugged. "Maybe."

They both laughed. "I couldn't help but notice you caught the bouquet after the ceremony."

Claudia waved him off. "Never mind that, don't look too deep into it."

"Then that would take all the fun out of things, wouldn't it?"

Claudia couldn't deny Christopher had a sense of swagger. A bit of old school swagger, but swagger nonetheless. Now she saw where Jaden got it from.

"That's all it is, fun and games. If I started believing old wives' tales, I just might lose my marbles," Claudia said.

Humor sat across his lips, "Ah, but there is something to be said about old wives' tales."

"Well, you do know more than me," Claudia admitted.

Christopher's broad smile lit up the room. "So you should listen to me, right?"

Claudia dipped her head in agreement.

"Are you dating someone currently, Claudia?"

Where she shouldn't have been surprised by his question, it had still taken her back.

"Um, well," she stumbled, "No, not really."

"Not really?" Christopher's smile turned into a questionable frown.

"Well I mean, no. I have a few prospects but nothing promising."

"I see." Christopher twirled her out from him than back in. "If none of those prospects are a part of this family, then you should just forget 'em."

Claudia openly gawked. "And why is that Mr. Rose?" Humor laced her voice.

"There are plenty of single men raised well here. No need to waste time with anyone else."

"Would that please you, Mr. Rose?"

Christopher's smile returned. "It would indeed. More grandbabies." He wiggled his brows and Claudia fell into a heap of laughter.

When her chuckles resided, she said, "Well, we can pretend for now can't we?"

"There may not be a need to pretend when you've already caught my son's eye."

Claudia's brows shot up. "Wha- what're you talking about?"

Christopher twirled Claudia again stopping her mid twirl. From across the room, dark eyes met hers and that intense heat wave that always overcame her soaked Claudia. She was certain she shivered under his heavy observation.

"Jesus," she whispered.

Octavia Davenport glided up to Jaden pulling his attention away. It was the escape Claudia needed. She turned quickly but was stuck with Christopher's knowing look.

"See, now someone else has his eye," Claudia stated.

"It's okay," Christopher said, "You can fight it for now, but if I know my son, and I think I do, it won't be long."

What was with the men in this family? Claudia thought. What was this thing she was supposedly fighting? But, Claudia knew, even though she'd never admit it.

Watching her from what felt like light years away, Jaden was a statue. Why he was so taken by Claudia Steven's was yet to be determined, but it was his undertaking to find out. Since the moment they'd met at the March of Dimes gala, Jaden knew there was something there. But even then, he hadn't understood it.

The powerful attraction to her was much more than it had been with any other woman in his life. It was magnetic, unrestrained and destabilizing. The more times he saw her, the more intense those feelings became. There had been many nights of conversations about her mother's care and the toll it had taken on Claudia to be deserted by her sister. Claudia never spoke about the rift between them, but he wanted her to release that when she was ready.

Their conversations delved into her partnership with Samiyah Manhattan at S & M Financial Advisory, and how they'd started their small business. Jaden let her speak about anything she was willing to discuss, revealing little about himself.

When Jaden asked her about her relationship with men, Claudia responded, "What would you like to know?"

"Why are you single, Claudia?"

She'd sighed. "I always found it interesting when men ask me that. How should I know? No one wants me I guess." She'd chuckled it off, but Jaden hadn't found the comment, whimsical. When his silence continued, Claudia spoke again. "Maybe I'm damaged goods, and at this time in my life, I don't want someone unstable or only searching for a good time."

Jaden had laid on his back that night with an arm behind his head and the phone to his ear listening to her words. He'd decided to keep his distance after that, not wanting to rush anything with her. Mostly because he wasn't sure which category he fell in. When it came to his business life, he was everything but unstable. But when it came to his personal life, Jaden was in no hurry to settle down. So in retrospect, Claudia was speaking directly to him, and Jaden knew she deserved better.

That was four months ago, and now he couldn't seem to stop the protuberant thoughts of her. His father twirled her as they moved on the dance floor. Jaden wondered about their conversation, but kept his eyes on Claudia's movements. Her bodacious hips rotated with smooth conversion and the smile on her face widened at something his father said. The body hugging dress pushed her breasts forward just enough to tease but not spill over. Her brown legs stretched to the floor into a pair of 'fuck me now' heels. Jaden was becoming a furnace as he watched her move.

Just when Jaden thought he could get away with undressing her with his eyes, his father twirled her again, and their eyes met. The moment was endless with a seductive gaze falling over Claudia's face. Jaden reached to loosen his tie when he realized he wasn't wearing one. *Shit,* she was flustering him. Their connection seemed to go on forever until Octavia Davenport called his name.

"Jaden, right?"

Jaden almost ignored her; unwilling to take his vision from Claudia. "Yes, and you're Octavia, right?" Finally, he turned his attention to Octavia.

"Yes, Claudia and Samiyah's employee."

Jaden slightly frowned. "I don't remember Claudia or Samiyah introducing you that way."

Octavia gave a soft smile. "It's because they think of me more as a co-worker than an employee. But it's one in the same I guess."

Jaden heard her, but his attention remained with Claudia. When he cast a glance back to Claudia, she was back in full swing with his father. The music changed, and Octavia lingered without as much as another word.

Being a gentleman, Jaden asked, "Would you like to dance, Mrs. Davenport?"

"Its Ms. Davenport, and you don't have to be so formal with me, Jaden. Call me Octavia."

He offered her a half smile. "Okay, Octavia, would you like to dance?"

"Sure, I thought you'd never ask."

Jaden was accustomed to women approaching him, but it never seemed to turn him on the way one would think. Jaden was a chaser, wanting to hunt his prey like the animal he was. But this proved to be difficult with his celebrity status in Chicago, and for that reason, he rarely enjoyed the attention.

Offering her his hand, Jaden and Octavia cruised to the dance floor. The upbeat tempo had everyone moving in a quick step. Jaden and Octavia were no different. As they moved, Jaden's thoughts ventured back to Claudia. She'd seemed hesitant about being around him tonight which was different from the previous moments they'd shared in one another's company.

Jaden needed to know what it was about. Claudia said the wedding was doing strange things to her, but why would that involve the way she reacted to him? He'd never gotten a chance to ask because she fled so quickly. Jaden wanted to believe it was because Claudia felt the same strong desire and it ruffled her feathers, but he couldn't be sure. Another part of him wondered if she was uninterested. That would be a first, but it wouldn't surprise him that the woman he finally set his sights on exploring more than just a physical relationship with, didn't want the same in return. Oh, the irony.

The weight of his thoughts battered him down, and although it was Octavia that Jaden twirled and two stepped around, it was Claudia that he wanted. Desperately. When the music changed, and a slow tempo sailed from the band, Octavia smiled sheepishly. Jonathon, Jaden's brother, approached them.

"Hey bro," Jonathon's eyes were fixated on Octavia, but he spoke to Jaden. "Do you mind if I cut in?"

Jaden smirked. "Do yah thing brother." Jaden punched him softly in the arm stepping to the side and Jonathon took his place, giving Jaden the opportunity to seek out the one he wanted. It was a welcomed pardon since Jaden didn't want to be rude to Octavia. But for this slow dance, Jaden wanted Claudia in his arms. He needed to feel the silkiness of her skin again. When he neared, Christopher twirled Claudia out releasing her at once and bringing her face to face with Jaden.

Her mouth opened in surprise and her palms rested against his broad chest catching her balance. His arms circled her immediately. "You're good," Jaden's thick vocals beat. "I've got you."

A faint smile crossed her lips. "It would seem so. I didn't see you, where'd you come from?"

"I've been with you this whole time. You didn't feel me?"

Claudia's belly flopped, and a flush of heat warmed her. She chuckled, "You sure do have a way with words, Mr. Rose."

His grin was mischievous. "I want you to call me Mr. Rose when I have you..." Jaden paused he wanted to tell her everything he wanted to do to her, but Jaden wasn't sure if that was the right move. Especially after her hesitation on the beach.

Claudia swallowed the lump in her throat. "You were saying," she asked seeking courage.

Jaden's grin spread into a suave smile. "I'll tell you later."

"Later?"

"Mmhmm."

"What makes you think there will be a later?"

"I'm hopeful."

Claudia's heart rate increased. She was hyperaware of his muscled chest pressed against her now hard nipples. His solid thighs laced between hers as if they were about to dance a dutty wine. More than anything, Claudia was attuned to his unyielding erection that seemed to extend past the standard length. Her body was screaming at this point, and Claudia was all set to immerse herself in the pleasure that he would most certainly provide.

Chapter Three

"You know your room comes with the wedding package."

Claudia turned around, and a smile spread across her face.

"Nah, we're going to do it right here on the dance floor," Claudia joked.

Samiyah threw her head back and laughed. But Jaden seemed to grow even harder. His eyes never left Claudia as she spoke to her best friend.

"Besides, I didn't think you'd notice, Mrs. Rose."

"Mmmm, sounds good, too," Samiyah cajoled. "Baby, do you mind giving Claudia and me a moment?"

"I do," Jonas said, "I mind it very much."

The ladies guffawed.

"I think Jaden minds it, too," Jonas looked at Jaden. "Am I right, brother?"

"Yes," Jaden ground out, "more than you've ever been in your life."

The ladies laughed again.

"We'll you'll have me forever, babe," Samiyah said. "And Jaden, well... we'll see."

Claudia pursed her lips. "You are too much!" Claudia waved at Samiyah and put her sight back on Jaden. "You don't mind, do you?"

"I've already answered that question woman."

"Awe, I'll be back." Her hand caressed his face, and a visible shudder fled through him. Claudia wiggled from his grasp. It was all she could do to keep from crushing her lips to his soft sexy mouth and saying to hell with all reason.

Claudia slid her arm through Samiyah's, removing her from Jonas's grasp.

"Men," Claudia said. "So controlling" she joked.

"Don't act like you don't love it," Jonas retorted.

"Maybe just a little," Claudia said setting her sights back on Jaden.

The ladies sashayed away with the men staring after them. Jonas spoke to Jaden, "Are you serious, bruh?"

Jaden didn't take his eyes off of Claudia. "Serious about what?"

Jonas snapped a finger in his face effectively bringing Jaden's gaze away from Claudia's backside. "Are you serious about her?"

"I still don't know what you mean."

"I think you do."

Jaden waited a beat. "I don't know what I am. Still trying to figure that out."

"You should probably do that before you go after her."

"What are you, Claudia's big brother?"

Jonas tapped him on his chest with the back of his hand. "I am now."

Jaden smirked. "I envy you."

"Don't, your time is coming."

Jaden wasn't so sure. He turned back to look for the girls but didn't find them.

"Look at you, I've never seen you go after someone like you've done tonight."

Jaden's brows creased and he slid his hands into his pockets. "I don't usually have to, and Claudia isn't making it easy."

"Is that why you're going after her, for the chase?"

Jaden pondered on his brother's words still unsure.

"You should pump your brakes. When you know without a shadow of a doubt what you want, then you go hard."

Jaden rubbed his chin. "Spoken from experience?"

"You know it."

"If this is the end result, then maybe I should just go hard."

"But is this what you want?"

Jaden didn't know if he wanted marriage. But he knew he wanted Claudia.

Away from eyes and ears, Samiyah and Claudia exited the tent relieving themselves of the expensive shoes on their feet.

"Are you having fun?" Claudia asked her.

Samiyah beamed. "Girl, I'm having the time of my life."

"Oooh you lucky, lucky girl!" They laughed.

"Seems like you may get a little lucky yourself."

"Hmmm," Claudia said.

Samiyah stopped walking and turned to her friend. "What's that about? You're usually excited to be around Jaden."

Claudia diverted her attention to the shore. "I still am."

Samiyah wasn't convinced. "Spill it."

Claudia exhaled deeply, "I don't know, I guess, I don't really know Jaden. As much as we've spoken in the past, he hasn't divulged much about himself. Besides that, I don't know if whatever this is we're doing has any legs. And," she added, "If it does have legs, I'm not sure if we should be together."

"First, don't take it too hard that he isn't letting you right in. Jonas did that to me in the beginning, and I called him out on it."

"Did you?"

"Yes, because I needed to know, but at that time we were both in agreement that trying a relationship was what we wanted to do. So my advice to you is, have a conversation with Jaden and see where this thing is going. Then call him out on his silence. Tell him to let you in."

"I don't know," Claudia waned.

"Why don't you know?"

"I'm not his type."

Samiyah's hands rested on her ample hips. "Excuse me."

Claudia smirked and rolled her eyes. "Let's not get into this okay, it's your wedding night. We should be talking about where you and that sexy man are going for the honeymoon. I know he wanted to keep it a surprise, but I also know he gives you what you want, so tell me so we can squeal together."

Samiyah regained her smile. "You don't get off the hook that easy. I'll tell you when you tell me what that last comment was all about."

Claudia sighed, "Oh come on, Samiyah!" Claudia twirled in the sand making herself dizzy before coming to a stop.

"What is this nonsense you're talking about?" Samiyah said.

"You know I'm not his type. You've seen the women he's been with."

"Tall, thin, supermodel features, is that what you mean?"

"Exactly!" Claudia said it like she'd won something. "You catch my drift then."

Samiyah nodded. "I do, but I can also tell you, those women are never the ones that seal the deal, if you know what I mean."

"Oh hush, you could be a supermodel if you applied yourself."

Samiyah's eyes balked. "Says who?"

"Says that fine ass man who didn't want to let you off the dance floor girl and can you blame him, you're killing it in this dress!"

Claudia held her hands up motioning them down into a coke bottle shape for added effect.

Samiyah laughed. "My guy's pretty awesome."

"Yes, he is," Claudia agreed. "And one day, so will mine."

The happiness in Claudia's voice dipped, and Samiyah noticed.

"Listen, girl, don't you dare hold yourself back because you think you're not his type. That is not the person you are. And if I have to remind you of this constantly? I will. Everyday!" Samiyah chimed. "Well, except while I'm on my honeymoon. You'll have to remind your own self during that time."

The women chuckled, and Claudia threw her arms around Samiyah. "I love you, girl.

"I love you, too."

"Don't look now."

"What?" Samiyah inquired.

"There are two dangerously gorgeous men walking our way. Samiyah twirled to a stop and the women watched the sexy men traipse toward them. Absentmindedly, Claudia lifted a hand and began to fan.

She leaned into Samiyah and whispered, "If Jaden keeps trying me, Im'ma end up pregnant tonight."

Samiyah let out a shrill of laughter and doubled over. Claudia's smile was bright and inviting. As Jaden neared, she slipped her tongue through her teeth and softly bit down. Next time he made a move she was going with it. No holds barred. The mantra repeated in her thoughts. She wouldn't let her head get in the way again. At least as long as they were in San Juan, Puerto Rico. This was the vacation of a lifetime, and if it were left up to Claudia, she wouldn't let her childish fears get in the way.

Chapter Four

Jaden and Jonas strolled to a stop before Claudia and Samiyah.

"Couldn't keep away, huh?" Claudia said to Jonas.

"Never," he responded with his gaze on his beautiful wife. Samiyah was still bent over laughing at Claudia's last comment.

"What's your excuse?" Claudia posed the question to Jaden.

"Who said I needed an excuse? I merely wanted to spend as much time with you on this beautiful island as possible."

"Why? So you can violate me?" She wiggled her eyes suggestively.

"Would you like that, Claudia?"

He stepped closer to her. Her nipples hardened again.

"Would you?" She countered.

Jaden held her with a piercing stare, his body temperature going from warm to molten. It was all he could take. Closing the distance, Jaden's mouth pushed against hers slow and inviting. Claudia's arms curled around his neck. A hot cinnamon flavor caressed her palate, and she moaned against his lips.

"Mmmmm."

Jaden's toned arms slid around her waist and up her back. He pulled her deeper, his fingers finding the round grooves of her bottom. Claudia's leg lifted to his waist.

"As I told you before, we have rooms," Samiyah said.

"Mmhmm," Jonas agreed. "And they're paid for, so you guys should think about using them."

Jaden was nearly too far away to give a damn. Tearing his mouth from hers Jaden spoke, "There's nothing like a little love on the beach."

"Yes," Claudia agreed before she had a chance to think clearly.

A wickedly prodigious smile danced across his moist lips. Without warning, Jaden lifted Claudia tossing her over his shoulder. She squealed, and Jonas and Samiyah laughed shaking their heads.

"Should we be worried?" Samiyah inquired.

"Nah," Jonas' responded. "They're both capable of making the right decisions, don't you think?"

Samiyah laid her head against Jonas chest. "You're right."

"Of course, I am."

The newlywed couple traipsed further down the beach in the opposite direction, set on having their own sexual display in the glow of moonlight.

Four days later

Enough

The Canon Image Class copier sent invoice after invoice sliding out of the printing machine one after the other. Claudia stood before it waiting patiently to gather her files and put them in their respective records. It was early Tuesday morning, and she'd come into work with a spring in her step. The weekend in San Juan went better than expected and Claudia arrived in Chicago two days ago. Thoughts of Jaden were at the front of her mind.

She hadn't heard from him since returning from Puerto Rico, and it was something Claudia wanted to get used to. No matter how much she told herself she was better off. To be consumed by a man like Jaden would probably send her on a path to a broken heart. Specifically, because he was a playboy. But she couldn't help but mull over the way his hands expertly caressed her skin. The way his skilled mouth landed in every crevasse her body owned. The way his muscular thighs felt behind hers. The exquisite torture of his sex thrusting into her heated core. Claudia squirmed standing at the machine trying to regain her composure. But it was no use. Jaden hadn't left her mind, and no matter how much she tried to tell herself it was just sex, Claudia knew it was so much more than that.

When she'd awakened the next day in Puerto Rico to an empty bed, the disappointment Claudia felt was substantial. But what had she expected exactly?

"A girl can only wish," she spoke to herself.

"Tell me about this wish?" A voice spoke.

Claudia turned full circle to find Octavia Davenport standing in her doorway.

"Knock much?" Claudia retorted.

"Sorry," Octavia said sheepishly, "I was getting ready to knock, but I saw the door open."

Claudia exhaled a deep breath. "You're fine. I'm sorry didn't mean to snap."

"I wouldn't call that a snap, but you're good. What's wrong? Anything I can help with?"

Claudia compressed her lips. "Unfortunately no. I'm grateful for the interruption. It's past time for me to get my head out of the clouds."

A sly smile spread across Octavia's lips. "Would it have anything to do with one of those to die for Rose brothers? Because if so, I can definitely understand."

Claudia's mind went back to the moment she saw Jaden on the dance floor with Octavia. She pretended like she didn't see him coming, but the truth of the matter was, she'd observed his every step.

"They have you under their spell, too?" Claudia asked.

Octavia laughed, her curly afro bobbing as her amusement increased. "Yeah," she spoke. "That Jonathon may be a one of a kind."

Claudia was relieved that Octavia had set her sights on another brother. She didn't know how she would feel otherwise.

"I think they're all one of a kind. Brothers, but definitely different. Are you and Jonathon going out?"

Octavia twisted her lips back and forth while she thought. "I wouldn't say we're going out, but he has asked me on a date."

"Mmmm," Claudia said waving her deeper into the office. "Why don't you have a seat and give me the details. I'd love to take my mind off Jaden."

"No, you wouldn't."

They chuckled. Octavia took a seat. "Jonathon seems to think, we've met before. But I would remember a man like him."

"Are you sure? I know you're a hot commodity these days. I've seen what, three good looking men come in to take you to lunch?"

Octavia giggled. "What can I say, I'm young and full of fun."

The ladies laughed again.

"Sure you are, and you're right to mingle. No need to look for anything serious."

Octavia nodded. "Well, Jonathon will be the fifth man you see take me out to lunch. And although I'm having fun right now, I'm not stupid enough to let a catch like Jonathon get past me."

"How do you know he's a catch?" Claudia asked. "Just because Rose is a household name doesn't mean he isn't a dog. If anything, those are the ones you have to be most careful about because they can have anyone they want."

"I don't know," Octavia mused. "Jonathon doesn't seem like the type. But I guess the only way for me to know for sure is after a few dates."

"It will take more than a few dates to find that out."

"It didn't for Samiyah."

Claudia thought about Octavia's statement. It was true. Samiyah and Jonas fell hard for each other quickly. It had taken all of two months for Jonas to propose. The ink on Samiyah's divorce from her previous marriage had barely dried.

"I guess you're right about that." Claudia shrugged, "What do I know? Go with your heart girl."

"That I plan to do. Do you need me to file those papers?"

There was a knock at the door, and both ladies looked up.

"Delivery for Claudia Stevens," Selena Strauss said walking into the room with a bouquet of pink and white long stem roses.

Claudia blushed, smitten by the generous gift. "For moi?"

The bundle of flowers was so extravagant you couldn't see Selena's face as she held them in front of her. Selena sat them down on Claudia's desk.

"Yes, they are for you, and I was almost nosey enough to open your card and see who they're from," she chuckled.

Claudia leaned her nose into the beautiful roses and inhaled. Reaching between the stems, she plucked the note and read the words scribbled across in refined letters.

Thinking of you on this beautiful day. If you'll have me, meet me at The Garden on 76th and Gladens tonight at 6 p.m.

If you don't show, I'll understand. J.

34

"What does it say?" Octavia and Selena asked, leaning over trying to get a glimpse of the words.

Claudia smiled tucking the card inside her bra. "That's for me to know and for you to never find out." A throaty laugh escaped her.

"Oh come on!" Octavia said. Selena was shaking her head, lips twisted.

"You're wrong for that," Selena countered.

"What?"

"After I spilled my date with Jonathon to you, this is how you do me?" Octavia said.

Claudia poked her lip out in a playful frown.

"Date with Jonathon? Rose?" Selena glanced from Octavia to Claudia. "Wait, what did I miss?"

Claudia chuckled and sauntered to the copier lifting the papers she'd printed. Walking back to Octavia and Selena, she divided the mound between the two.

"There's plenty for you two to file for the next couple of hours before closing time. I suggest you get to work."

Octavia shook her head slowly. "You're cold, you know that?"

Claudia shrugged, "I don't know what you're talking about."

"Un huh, you wouldn't do Samiyah like this."

Claudia rolled her eyes. They were both right, but Samiyah was her home girl, these two busybodies weren't.

"I still love you though," Claudia said.

Octavia rose to her feet. "I don't think you do," she teased taking a stack of the papers and sashaying out of the office.

Chapter Five

The Garden restaurant held one of Chicago's most expensive upscale dining experiences. With its crafted rose bushes that decorated the walkway, to its handpicked seafood that arrived daily, fresh, and ready to be grilled. Claudia sauntered through the open entrance, scanning the fine drapery and luxurious surroundings with her dark brown eyes.

With her tresses freshly washed and conditioned, and her foundation bringing out the depth in her potent features, Claudia was feeling herself. Never mind the dress she wore was thin and framed to every curve she owned.

"Welcome to the Garden," a hostess approached. "Can I help you to a seat, madam?"

"I'm with someone, Jaden Alexander Rose?"

The hostess' eyes stretched in surprise. It was no doubt she knew who Jaden was, everyone in Chicago did. But before the hostess could respond, a flash of lights behind Claudia caught her attention along with everyone else's. Turning toward the commotion revealed a black Lamborghini Huracan Coupe with chrome wheels. The sports car had barely spun to a stop before bulbs popped from nearby paparazzi that lie in wait for a celebrity appearance. The driver side door rose slowly, and Jaden stepped out, fastening a lone button on his suit jacket. Claudia watched in mesmerized adoration as he strolled toward her moving with methodical strides as the bulbs continued to flash. The jacket did nothing to hide his muscular physique, and Claudia's eyes roamed from his Brioni shoes up his tailored suit to the robust column of his neck. Jaden's smooth movements brought him through the open doors to stand firmly before Claudia, and he had no idea of the dangerous beat of her pulse upon his nearness.

"Mi Amor, I'm sorry for the tardiness. If it is your wish to leave, I'll understand, but I hope like hell you stay." His fathomless golden-brown eyes dug a hole into her, beckoning Claudia to succumb to his plea.

Claudia swallowed back the swelling in her throat and silently shook herself. "I just arrived, so you're okay. Let's find a seat."

Jaden offered her a charming smile and spoke to the hostess. "We have reservations, Rose."

"I have your reservations here, sir, if you'll follow me."

Claudia turned and Jaden placed his hand at the small of her back as they meandered through the restaurant. At their table, Jaden pulled her seat and allowed her to sit before claiming his chair.

"I apologize for the paparazzi."

Claudia shrugged. "Comes with the territory, right?"

"Unfortunately."

A waitress strutted forward handing them menus.

"Give us a minute," Jaden said.

"Yes sir," the waitress walked away.

Jaden's gaze followed the outline of Claudia's soft face. "Mi Amor, you're absolutely beautiful tonight." He reached out to touch her chin. "I can never keep my hands to myself around you." He pulled his bottom lip between his teeth before releasing it. "I wonder why that is."

The throbbing sex between Claudia's thighs caused her to squeeze her legs tight. She would have to be careful with Jaden, or he would make her fall head over heels in love, and that would be a disaster.

"I'm not sure, Jaden, but when you find out, I'm intrigued to know the details."

Jaden's lips spread into a vibrant smile.

"Thanks for dinner. I wasn't expecting the lovely bouquet of roses. They have my office smelling like a spring garden."

Jaden rubbed his chin offering up a lazy grin. "I've been trying to come up with a way to ask you out. Contrary to popular belief, it's not something I often do."

Claudia's brows rose. "No?"

"Afraid not."

"Hmmm, why now?"

"I enjoy spending time with you, Claudia, and I hope you don't mind if I bother you more often."

She surely didn't mind. Not one iota.

"I'm having fun with you also, Jaden, but you don't have to showcase me to get into my bed. Neither do you have to send me roses to get my attention. We've already been there. Just call, I know this is not your thing."

Jaden sat back in the seat, his vision never leaving Claudia. The intensity of his gaze usually warmed her from head to toe, but now it only ruffled her feathers.

"I think you have me mistaken, chérie. I'm not doing this to get you into bed at all."

"No?"

"No."

"Then why are you doing it?"

When he didn't respond fast enough Claudia went on. "Did you not hope the evening would end with a night cap?"

"Not necessarily—"

"Do you not want to feel yourself thrusting into me like when we were in Puerto Rico? Have you not had thoughts about us and wanted to revisit the pleasure we both experienced with one another?"

Jaden was slow with his words when he spoke.

"That is not the purpose of this date."

Claudia peered at him. Why else would he be engaging her if not to get back in her bed?

"You don't have to lie to me, Jaden, its fine. Let's just skip the 'date'. Claudia said it like it was fictional. "And go straight to a hotel. I won't feel slighted, I promise."

Claudia rose to her feet and Jaden reached forward, his hand covering hers. "Please," he said, "sit."

They considered each other for a long drawn out moment before Claudia sat slowly in her seat.

"Is there a problem?" she asked.

Disconcerted, Jaden spoke. "Is that how you want things to be between us, Claudia?"

Claudia wouldn't dare tell him her dreams of them together in a budding relationship; of them making love and having babies; of them as husband and wife. Silly thoughts like that permeated her mind daily, but they were only for her.

"What else is there?"

The waitress bounced back to their table, interrupting their awkward conversation.

"Are you ready to order?"

"Yes," Claudia said. "I'll have whatever he's having." She looked to him expectantly. But Jaden was still trying to figure her out.

"We'll have your shrimp and parmesan steak entrée."

"Anything to drink?"

"Water for me," Claudia injected.

"Water for us both," Jaden confirmed.

"Right away," the waitress said.

"I apologize if I've come off as if all I want from you is sex. You need to know, what we had in Puerto Rico wasn't just sex. The connection we share is eternal. It goes beyond something so fleeting as mindless sex. I want to know you, Claudia, in every way imaginable."

Claudia was stomped. Although she heard his words, they rattled around her brain loosely, and she was having a hard time trying to understand his meaning. If the sudden squeeze of her brows was any indicator of this, he didn't say. Instead, he let her mull it over.

Jaden was not a man to play tedious games. He'd been raised by a firm but loving father, and although he was young when his mother passed, whenever his father would reference his mother, Jaden could sense the love they shared. Never would he contemplate mistreating women. It would be an embarrassment to the Rose name and his integrity.

"I see," Claudia said finally.

"Do you?"

She smiled coquettishly. "Yes, I think I've embarrassed myself."

A chuckled left him. "Don't be, it's quite alright. With everything, I'm sure you've seen in the papers and on TV, it would be easy to comprehend your misunderstanding."

Claudia breathed a sigh of relief. "So we're still friends then?"

"For now."

They watched each other, silently dissecting the conversation they had. Could it be possible, Claudia wondered, that he would be interested in a relationship? She shook the thoughts. That was the last thing she needed; to distract herself with thoughts of happily ever after. Those things don't happen to women like her.

She would be good to win a ticket with a lucky lottery scratch off, let alone be in a relationship with one of the Rose men. Comfortable that she'd shed some light on that train of thought, Claudia could bunker down and ride this wave of situationship until the very end. She was sure when looking back, it would be a mark in her history books she would never forget. And from here on out, she wouldn't ruin it by speaking too fast. She'd just let it play out.

Across the table, Jaden sat with his own thoughts. He was under the impression that his simple caresses and show of affection had given Claudia the notion he only wanted to be physical with her. Nothing could be further from the truth. Now he was making it his mission to show her otherwise. No matter how hard it would be to keep his hands to himself. It was true, Claudia was a sexy siren if he'd ever known one and he didn't think she knew it.

But if it was one thing Jaden was raised well on, it was showing a woman her worth. Claudia Stevens would know it after he was done and she would never forget it. Jaden pondered on his reasons for pursuing Claudia so intensely. He still wasn't sure. The attraction between them was compelling, and whenever she wasn't around, he found himself daydreaming about her.

It was almost psychotic. He may have to have a conversation with his father about that later. Jaden wasn't crazy nor did he have a need to be monogamous, but being around Claudia stirred his soul, and he needed to know why. Her silent behavior spoke as if she felt the same way, but her words went another direction. For now, Jaden would enjoy his time with Claudia and work out the kinks later. But first, he was set on showing her the time of her life. An idea came to mind, and a smile spread across his masculine face.

"Mmmm, what's that smile all about, Mr. Rose?" Claudia asked.

"By chance, do you like to dance, Claudia?"

Chapter Six

The Lamborghini Coupe pulled into a parking spot, and Jaden cut the growl of the engine. Claudia glanced to the sign that introduced the building.

"Let's Move Dance Studio?" Claudia asked, puzzled.

Jaden's smile curved into a devilish grin. "Have you ever taken lessons before?"

Claudia gave off a genuine laugh. "No, I haven't. We couldn't afford that sort of thing growing up."

"But you wanted to?"

Claudia poked her lip out in thought, her shoulders bouncing as she mused. "It probably would've kept me out of a lot of trouble," she chuckled.

Jaden opened his door and jumped out circling the Lamborghini to open Claudia's door. She slid out gliding into his embrace. They were face to face, she looking into his honey glazed irises.

"I don't have on the right clothes for this."

Jaden ran an appreciative eye over her thin sequin dress, to the four-inch stiletto's that boosted her poise. "I'd say, you're dressed perfectly for this occasion."

Claudia blushed and dropped her head. Jaden lifted her chin with a finger. "I love it when you look at me head on. I could get used to staring into the glow of your amber eyes." He laser gaze traced an outline around her face, "so beautiful." His hand fell over her ear giving it a gentle caress and tug.

Claudia blushed again and bit the corner of her lip. "You sure know how to make a woman feel good."

"It's the truth, chérie." Jaden took a step back and interlaced his fingers with hers. "Come, let's dance."

They strolled to the entrance and entered. The door chimed as they moved through. "I'm surprised they're still open."

"It isn't that late."

Claudia glanced at the time. "It 8:17."

"Okay, you got me, I called in a favor."

"Un huh, I knew it."

"You're not having second thoughts, are you?"

They continued to move down the hallway flanked with photographs of famous dancers and ballet stars.

"No, I'm good. I wanna see what you got."

Jaden paused. "What I got? Who said I could dance?"

Claudia giggled. "Well it was your idea to come here in the first place, so I guess I should've asked. Can you dance, Mr. Rose?"

They stepped into a dance hall surrounded with mirrors on the walls and hardwood floors.

"Good evening, Jaden, how are you? It's been a long time."

Jaden held a bright smile as the tall, thin Caucasian woman skated to his side to throw her arms around him. Claudia hadn't missed the informal tone of her greeting, and she wondered just how well the two knew each other.

Being a gentleman, Jaden threw a lone arm around the woman then slowly pulled away. "Cassie, I'd like you to meet, Claudia Stevens. Claudia this is Cassie Singapore. She's donated to my mom's foundation every year since her passing."

"How are you?" Claudia asked.

"I'm good, how are you?"

"In good hands," Claudia peeked at Jaden. "For now," she said repeating what Jaden said earlier.

"That you are," Cassie said giving Jaden a wink. "Well the studio is yours for the next hour. I've got to go pick up my dog from the babysitter, then I'll make my rounds and come back to lock up."

"How is Kasanova, anyway?" Jaden asked referring to the wiener dog.

"Better than ever, always eating."

They chuckled. "That's what dogs do most."

"You're right about that"

"I'll see you guys in a little bit."

"If she's leaving, who's going to teach us the dance moves?"

Jaden strolled to the stereo system with amusement in his eyes. After messing with the dial, a smooth jazz melody played.

"We're going to try just a few basic steps," he said.

Claudia smirked. "Aaa ha, you're going to teach me these moves, Mr. Rose?"

"You sound surprised, chérie."

Claudia sauntered deeper into the room and proceeded to take her heels off. "I've never known a man who could dance, I mean really dance."

"You'll find that I'm not like most men and you should leave your shoes on. The dance I'm about to teach you works best with the support."

Claudia had no doubt he was different than other men, and she wanted to know just how much. Jaden swayed to the music and slowly crossed the room to her. Reaching out, Jaden slid a strong arm around her waist pulling Claudia flush against his chest. With the other hand, he interlocked their fingers.

"This dance calls for us to be intimate."

Claudia's brows rose.

"By intimate, I mean close," Jaden smirked. "Your movements should mirror mine. When we touch, our connection should be as if we're one. I am an extension of you and vice versa. So wherever I go," he took a step back, and Claudia moved forward; their thighs causing friction as they stirred. "You go." He smiled at her ability to learn fast.

"Like this?" she spoke. Her voice was low just above a whisper.

Jaden spun her out and tugged her hand, and Claudia twirled back into his embrace. "Just like that," he confirmed.

His lips were a breath away from hers, and the temperature in the room warmed. The music continued to serenade them, and Jaden moved in slow steps.

Gliding to the right in sync, their bodies caused nerve endings to spark and flutter across one another's skin.

"To execute this dance perfectly, confidence must ooze from your body language. Your posture upright," Jaden said, watching Claudia straighten her shoulders, "your head held high," he continued. Claudia's eyes lifted to meet his. It was hard for her to stay that way. Jaden's undeniable charm made her heart flutter when looking into the depths of his eyes. She could never hold his gaze for long, her head always fell.

But now in this moment, she followed his instructions wanting to learn something new from him.

"Yes," his dark voice beat. "Like that."

They moved together, Claudia following his steps. "Keep your chest elevated and spine straight. It helps your core remain strong."

Being so close to Jaden with his instructions was driving her libido crazy. Claudia was officially turned on. Hell, she'd been turned on since he pulled to the front of The Garden in his sports car. But this was visceral in a way she'd never thought of intimacy. Her belly flip flopped as her nipples pushed against the firmness of his broad chest. Suddenly, she gained confidence, and this time when Jaden spun Claudia out, her hand went into the air along with her chin.

When he pulled back, she went gently and charismatic with the grace of a ballroom dancer. Jaden was right; the stilettos boosted her movements. They were ideal for the twirls and quick movements. Jaden stepped forward with a left foot, and Claudia glided back with her right. When Jaden stepped forward with his right, Claudia stepped backward with her left.

"Yes," he said. A pleasant smile highlighted his lips. "Now we rock," he held her, "back and forth." With his legs apart, Jaden juggled weight from one foot to the other without taking a step, moving them softly to the rhythm.

"Feel the pace of the song. Sway with it, move with it. The music is also an extension of us both. Like a vine, we move and unravel with it as we also fold and bend to its allure."

Claudia had never felt this good while dancing. At most, she'd needed to be intoxicated to get on the dance floor in any club to put her best foot forward and still then she was never as confident as she was now. Gliding with Jaden to this music seemed so normal. And Claudia really felt like an extension of him.

"You're a fast learner," Jaden acknowledged.

"You're a fantastic teacher. I like how you take your time with your student. Have you ever thought about making this a profession?"

Jaden chuckled. "These are only the basics, chérie. I'd have to have a little bit more style to call it a profession."

Claudia pressed her lips together. Somehow she knew Jaden was being coy and that he indeed had the style he spoke of.

"No need to be shy now, you've shown your hand."

"Have I?"

"Yes."

"Are you sure about that?"

Claudia giggled and Jaden dipped her with a sway of motion before pulling her back flank against his chest.

He continued to instruct her, taking two slow steps then rocking side to side. "Step, step, now rock."

Claudia was feeling like a professional herself. That was just the self-assurance that exuded from her bones.

"On the second step, turn out to your side. I'm going to release you. Once I do, make the move your own. I'll come back to reclaim you, and that's when the dance gets a bit more intense."

Claudia arched a brow. Didn't he know this dance was already intense? As if reading her thoughts, he spoke. "More."

A furnace was the only thing that could describe the temperature of her body at the moment. Claudia inhaled and exhaled a deep breath. Their feet moved, and on the second step, Claudia turned her torso to the side. Simultaneously, Jaden released her and she swiveled to a stop. With her hands, Claudia slid them up the side of her hips while rotating them in a sensual wine as her fingers rode to her breasts.

Jaden's gaze darkened and he stalked her with each step; a rhythmic flow in his movements. When he was in arms reach, Claudia held her arms out to him continuing to circle her hips. With ferocity, Jaden pulled her back, and she twirled twice before running into the brick wall that was his chest. With their legs now mixing and mingling, they ground into each other, pelvis to pelvis. Claudia's heart was slamming against her chest, and she shakily gazed back into Jaden's golden-brown eyes.

Jaden's barely restrained willpower was hanging on by a thread. His erection was palpable, pushing against his pants with strained fury.

"How am I doing so far?" Claudia asked now breathless.

Jaden's voice was rough and dark when he spoke. "Like you've been doing this all your life. Are you sure you haven't had lessons?"

Claudia smiled. "I'm certain. I couldn't forget a dance like this."

Jaden tipped his head in agreement.

"I know you've had your fair share of partner's," Claudia began.

He gave her an inquisitive look.

"Dance partners I mean."

"Not as many as you would assume."

"Were any of them as intense as this?"

"Not even close."

Claudia registered a smiled and dipped her head. "Somehow I find that hard to believe."

"Why is that?" Jaden's voice saturated her bones, coating her in a trail of chills that seemed to go on forever. Claudia shivered in his arms.

"With you being anybody's teacher, a dance like this could only get," she searched for a word before landing on, "hotter."

Dark laughter low and gritty slid from his throat.

"Are you hot, Claudia?"

"Hell yes."

Jaden laughed again. The timbre of his vocals sending another wave of heat through her. The music faded out, and Claudia pulled apart from him. It was all she could do to keep from melting where she stood. Her panties were drenched and her body awakened. What would she do with this man? Jaden said he wanted to get to know her. But could she be friends with him? Lord knows Claudia was having a hard-enough time as it was in his presence.

In the past, Claudia and Jaden had been around each other sporadically. No doubt whenever their paths crossed it was intense. But the times apart from him were lengthier. It gave Claudia time to check herself. A man like Jaden Alexander Rose would have her doing things she'd never considered, like dancing in a studio at 8 o'clock at night. With that last thought, Claudia checked the time. It was 9:40.

"I hate to cut this short, but I need to leave."

Jaden strolled to the stereo and turned it off. "Is everything alright?"

"Yes, it's just," Claudia sent her fingers through her hair. She'd spoken briefly about her mom but not in detail.

Jaden approached her. "What is it?"

"I have to check on my mother. Sometimes she forgets to take her medicine."

"Say no more."

Jaden pulled out his cell and made a phone call.

"Hey, are you done?" Cassie answered.

"Yes, but I didn't want to leave the studio open."

"There's a spare key on the table next to the piano."

Jaden's strides took him to the table, sure enough, there was a key there.

"If you'll just lock up for me, you can drop the keys off at my place."

. Jaden thought about her request. At this point he didn't have a choice. For a moment he wondered if leaving a spare key had been intentional. Years ago, he'd taken Cassie on a date that ended in her bedroom. It was a spur of the moment fluke like so many of his other escapades. However, Jaden had made it known he wasn't interested in anything more and Cassie acted as if she was fine with that.

Jaden hoped it wasn't a mistake to call Cassie, but whatever her intentions, Jaden would be as open and honest as he always was.

"I'll see you soon," he said disconnecting the call. Jaden set his sights on Claudia. "After you."

Chapter Seven

The Lamborghini pulled to valet, and Jaden handed the attendant Claudia's ticket. Back at The Garden, they sat and waited for her car to be pulled around front.

Claudia took another hand through her hair. "I had a great time." Her smile was soft and genuine.

"So did I. We'll have to put those newfound skills to use one day." He grinned.

A look of trepidation crossed Claudia's features. "You mean behind closed doors, right?"

Jaden chuckled. "No, I mean in front of the world."

Claudia shook her head. "That's never happening."

"Why not?"

"I'm not as brave as you, Jaden."

"Yes you are."

Claudia smiled, her teeth on full display as she shook her head. "No, I'm not," she giggled.

"We'll see."

"I guess we will."

The valet pulled to a stop next to the Lamborghini.

"So this means I'll see you again?" Jaden asked.

"I would love that."

Jaden's smile was full of relief then he opened the door making his way to her side. He pulled the handle, and the door sprang upwards. Jaden held his hand out, and Claudia accepted it standing to her feet. Once again, Jaden didn't move, instead holding her hostage inside the warm cocoon of his embrace.

Claudia went to speak but lost the nerve.

"What is it?" Jaden asked, his voice smooth and barbaric.

"Nothing," she gave a shy grin.

"Nah, you don't get to do that."

"Do what?"

"Backtrack." He detained her with a piercing gaze.

Claudia's tongue traced her teeth before she meshed her lips together.

"Don't hold back; you're free to say whatever you want with me."

A layer of chills ran the length of her. "The night doesn't have to end here," she said. "I just need to check on my mother than we could go..." her voice trailed off, "somewhere else."

Jaden knew what Claudia implied, and the bulge in his pants agreed, but his resolve held firm. Claudia had mistaken him for only wanting her between the sheets, and he was determined to show her otherwise.

Jaden took her hand in his and placed a soft, warm kiss on the back, his eyes never leaving hers. "As much as I would love that, chérie, I think it's best if we leave the night the way it is."

Claudia was feeling foolish again not knowing how to take his rejection. Jaden watched her eyes and saw the disappointment.

"I have wanted to do this all night though."

Jaden's arms moved up Claudia's back, his palm gripping her head as he pulled her mouth to his. The kiss was magical. Somewhere between a fairy tale and a dream. Soft lips sealed in a seductive caress that took Claudia to a breathtaking oblivion. Paparazzi jumped out of nowhere, crowding their space. Bulbs of light flashed as Jaden deepened the kiss.

Claudia's tongue slid in his mouth and sautéed with his tongue. The wet and warmth of their salsa felt like a free fall. It was only when a camera man stood between their personal space that Jaden pulled back. His hand shot out, and his brows knocked together in a frown as he shoved the disrespectful photographer back. The man stumbled and fell to the ground. With swiftness, Jaden stepped back, covering Claudia until she'd made it safely inside her Toyota.

Jaden shut the door and strolled back to the driver side of his Lamborghini sliding into the heated leather seats. He closed the door and dialed Claudia. She answered turning to look at him through her window.

"I apologize for the paparazzi," he said. "Lock your doors and drive straight home. Call me when you get there."

"Okay," was all she said before ending the call. Still breathless from such an explosive kiss, Claudia made an effort to gain her bearings. She put the car in drive and pulled away from the curve. Driving through the winding streets of downtown Chicago, her mind remained with him. Claudia could still taste the tang of his tongue and the suction of his lips. She closed her eyes briefly still trying to steady her fast-paced heart.

"Lord have mercy," she said out loud. This thing between them was undeniable, and Claudia wondered how she would ever let him go when the time came.

Opening the door to her mid-century modern home, Claudia glided through the entrance and hung her purse on the doorknob. The house was dark, and all was silent with the exception of a TV that quietly ran in a back room. Trying to shake off thoughts of Jaden, Claudia traipsed down the hallway, past the kitchen and living area to her mother's room. Sitting slumped on the couch, Adeline Stevens light snores whispered from her nose, and her glasses sat crooked on top of it.

In front of Adeline on the table was a half a glass of water and a single pill. Claudia exhaled a deep sigh. Her mother hadn't taken her blood pressure pill even after Claudia set the alarm to go off at 6:30 p.m., for Adeline. It seemed her mother was doing a lot of that these days. If Claudia weren't personally around to feed Adeline the pills, they'd never get taken, which frustrated Claudia more than anything.

The TV was stationed on the news channel, and the weatherman was talking about sunny skies tomorrow afternoon. Claudia went to her mother and rubbed a hand down her shoulder and back speaking gently.

"Mom."

Adeline stirred but didn't rise. Claudia shook her with a heavy hand.

"Mom."

"Humph, what is it?" Adeline responded with her eyes still closed.

"You didn't take your medicine."

Adeline's aging eyes crinkled then fluttered opened; the gray in her tendrils mashed to the side of her face. "Girl, you didn't wake me up about no medicine, did you, because that's just rude."

Claudia considered her for a moment. "It's rude not to take your medicine when that's what it's here for. You don't want to give your favorite child a heart attack if something happens to you because you failed to take it, do you?"

Adeline sighed and sat up straight, stretching her short arms as she yawned. "Chile, gone with the dramatics will you. Ain't nothing about to happen to me that God didn't plan. So whatever He wants, His will be done."

Claudia sat down slowly next to her mom. "Don't blame your stubbornness on God. These pills are here to help you, and deciding not to take them is taking the life God gave you for granted."

Claudia was good with turning the tables on her mom. Adeline always had a reference about God, but she only used them when they benefited her the most. Adeline waved her off. "You think you're cute with that little comment don't cha?"

Claudia grinned. "Come on, let me help you get into bed, and watch your step."

Adeline looked over her child. "I'm old, not senile."

"Of course, mama."

Adeline got to her feet with Claudia's help, and moseyed over to the queen size bed flanked with a Serta mattress that Adeline was adamant about getting; dubbing it the best sleeping mattress in the world.

After helping Adeline get comfortable, Claudia went back for the pill and the glass of water. "Take your medicine."

Adeline waved her off. "I don't need that. I'm going to sleep now, leave me alone."

"Mama, take your medicine." Claudia's voice rose, and Adeline peered at her.

"Who you raising your voice to, chile?"

Claudia slumped, defeated. "I didn't mean to raise my voice, mom. I just need you to please, take your medicine."

Adeline pursed her lips and sat up taking the glass of water and pill from Claudia's hand. Claudia watched carefully to make sure she swallowed before replacing her frown with a smile.

"Thank you, mama." She kissed Adeline on the cheek. "I love you."

"Yeah, yeah, you're welcome. How was your date?"

Thoughts of Jaden resurfaced, and Claudia's face glowed. "It went well."

"Does he have a job?"

"Yes, he has a job, mom."

"Does he have his own car?"

Claudia dropped her head in the palm of her hand and chuckled.

"What?" Adeline asked.

"Nothing, yes, he has a car and a house of his own. Anymore questions?"

Adeline's eyes rose in surprise. Finally, her daughter had managed to entertain a man who had some business about himself. Unless...

"Is he single?"

Claudia's mouth dropped. "Mama, what kind of home wrecker do you take me for?"

"I didn't call you that, you did. Just because he may be married doesn't mean you had to know about it. I'm just asking."

Claudia was shaking her head now. "There's no way I would tolerate a man that is married."

A small smile spread across Adeline's face. She reached out and patted Claudia's arm and laid back down. Claudia knew her mother thought of her the same way her sister, Desiree did, reckless. But she was set to prove them both wrong. She just didn't know how to go about it. Adeline turned to face the wall, getting comfortable under her covers.

Standing to her feet, Claudia strolled out the room. "I want to meet him," Adeline spoke up. Claudia's footsteps paused. She wanted to meet him? Jaden. Claudia closed her eyes and sighed. She would love for Jaden to meet her mother but he wasn't a boyfriend or even a possibility. They were just having fun, getting to know one another and building a friendship. *But those are the makings of a beautiful relationship.* No. Claudia shook her head. She couldn't. The disappointment she would most surely find in her mother's eyes after Jaden no longer came around would hurt more than finding pleasure in showing him off now.

Claudia proceeded to her bedroom when her phone chimed.

You didn't call me when you made it home. Am I to assume you are safe?

Claudia smiled and stuck her tongue between her teeth for a slight suck. She sent a text back;

I'm sorry, you're absolutely right. In my defense, I was caught up talking to my mom about you. She sent a smiley emoji.

Oh yeah, all good I hope.

Claudia typed back; **Absolutely, but I'm keeping it a secret.**

A few moments passed without a response. Claudia shed her shoes, clothes and headed for her master bathroom when a particular song rang out. Taking quick steps back to the smartphone, she scooped the phone up and answered.

"How can I help you, Mr. Rose?" Claudia sauntered back to the bathroom and paused leaning into the doorway.

"Sir," he said.

"Excuse me?"

"If you are going to be formal with me," his voice thundered. "It's how can I help you, sir."

A tiny smile formed on Claudia's face. "Okay, how can I help you... sir?"

Jaden's grin spread like a Cheshire cat. "That's my girl."

Claudia was experiencing all kinds of vibes right now. Her pulse had elevated, and her chocolate brown skin warmed. A simmering path of nerves settled amid her thighs and she squeezed them together.

"Now what were you saying about the conversation with your mother?"

"It's really not a big deal." Claudia meant to say it normally, but it came out throaty. Her body was in constant need of him ever since their rendezvous in Puerto Rico. And she was about ready to throw caution to the wind. After all, Claudia hadn't been very deterred up till this point. Why start now?

"Where are you?" She asked.

"Sitting in my car."

"Going someplace?"

He went silent for a moment. "I'm returning something to a friend."

That answer was vague and Claudia didn't like it. But why should she care?

"So what are you doing on the phone with me?"

"I wanted to hear your voice, chérie."

"Liar."

A deep sexy rumble escaped him. "A liar I am not, I also wanted to know about this correspondence between you and your mother that you are set on keeping a secret.

"You want to know that badly, huh?"

"I do."

Claudia's mind swirled with thoughts of I do. Again her eyes closed and she massaged her temples. How could she build a friendship with him if she couldn't keep thoughts of a romantic relationship from assailing her mind.

"She wants to meet you."

"Is that right?"

"Don't worry, I don't plan to drag you over here. I'll come up with something."

"Why, I would love to meet her."

Claudia's brow raised. "I don't think you understand. She's going to feel you out and question you to death like you're my high school prom date."

A dark rumble of laughter boomed from Jaden. "I think I can handle it."

"Yeah, but I don't think I can."

They chuckled. "You'll be fine. When would she like to meet me?"

"Next year. By then you'll have found someone to marry, and she can stop wondering about the guy I never brought home."

Their conversation went silent. Claudia glanced at the phone to see if he was still there. The timer ticking down indicated that he was.

"You know something I don't?" Jaden asked.

"I'm just," she sighed and mumbled, "speaking too fast again."

"We'll have to do something about that."

The indiscreet warning made her squirm, and Claudia's thoughts fled straight to the gutter.

"I need to call you back, chérie."

"I'm heading for a shower then climbing into bed. If you call and I don't answer, I'm already fast asleep."

Jaden imagined the dark chocolate glow of her legs, thighs and swollen breasts under the shower's waterfall. Keeping his hands to himself had proven difficult and staying out of her bed would present an even bigger challenge.

"How about I just give you a call tomorrow."

"That's fine."

"Good night, chérie."

"Good night."

Jaden sat his phone in the middle console of his Lamborghini. Now outside of Cassie's house, he reached for her studio key and left the car.

Chapter Eight

The door swung open revealing a pair of bare pearl legs. The thin nighty fell over Cassie's shoulders, but opened; exposing her bare stomach and see through lingerie bra and panties set.

Jaden had done exactly what she wanted, come to the lair. His eyes roved down to her bare pedicured feet, back up to her small pointy breasts. He tossed her key up, and she caught it as it neared.

"Sorry for the interruption," he said. "I would've been here sooner, but I had to take care of something first."

Cassie shrugged. "No need for the apology. I'm grateful you came all this way to return my key."

Jaden rubbed his jaw. "Yeah, about that." He placed his hands in his pocket. "You can be truthful with me Cassie, did you leave your key on purpose?"

Cassie gasped and covered her chest. "Why Jaden, are you asking if I set you up so I could get you over here and seduce you?"

Jaden thought better of her. "Never mind, forget I asked. Have a good night." He inclined his head and turned to take his leave.

"Wait!"

Jaden paused and looked back over his shoulder.

"Why don't you come in for a minute?"

Slowly turning full circle, Jaden kept his hands in his pockets as he spoke. "Now, why would I do that?" His voice was smoothed and unbothered.

"We're friends, right? It's been a long time. Let's catch up."

Jaden was starting to rethink taking back the ill intent thoughts before. He flipped his wrist and glanced at his watch. "It's late. I don't think that's such a good idea."

"Why is that? You have someone to go home to?"

No, he didn't, but he was working on it. After that thought crossed his mind, Jaden frowned. When exactly had he decided he was working on it?

"Let's be honest, Cassie. Nothing can come of us catching up, except for..."

A smile lingered at the corner of Cassie's pink lips; a gleam in her eye.

"Listen," Jaden spoke, "I appreciate you for opening your studio tonight. I owe you one. Have a good night."

He turned to walk away, and Cassie watched him go. If it was the chase Jaden wanted, it was what he'd get she surmised.

The next day Claudia walked into the doors of Morgan's on Fulton. A Caucasian male dressed down in a button-down shirt, black slacks and tie approached her.

"Can I help you with something?"

Claudia took a quick eye over the place. She'd scoured the internet for the perfect venue, and this seemed to be what she was searching for.

"I'm looking to rent your establishment for a fundraising benefit and would like to get a personal tour of the place."

"Tell me more about your event."

"I've started a nonprofit Caregivers Organization. The mission is to give back and be a light house, so to speak, for families who have full time or part time caregivers in the home. Caregivers Organization will be a resource for families, offering support groups, individual living assessments, training on medications and more. But I'm just starting up, so for now, I need a venue to help me get the ball rolling.

"I completely understand, and that sounds like a great nonprofit. How did you come up with the idea?"

"I happen to be a full-time caregiver myself, and in the beginning, I felt alone trying to find the resources I needed. Now I want to make sure no one within my reach feels the same way."

The man smiled. "Excellent, just excellent. Follow me, let me show you around."

They strolled through three large rooms; some with a lounge area holding sofa's, a bar, and floor to ceiling windows. Claudia's phone vibrated as they reached the last room and she frowned at the unknown number on her screen.

"Excuse me for a moment, please."

"No problem."

She stepped to the side and answered. "Hello?"

"Good morning, how are you?"

It was her sister, Desiree.

Claudia braced herself for a fight. It never failed with Desiree. She'd start out pleasant then turn into a tyrant.

"I'm fine, how about yourself?"

"I'm good. How's mom?" Desiree asked.

"Also, fine."

"I'm coming to see her this weekend."

Creases ran across Claudia's forehead. "Okay, will that be Friday, Saturday, or Sunday?"

"It will be Friday, and I'll be leaving out on Sunday."

"Staying for a full weekend this time, nice."

"If you have something to say, just say it. I don't want to fight with you in front of mom."

"Hey, I'm not looking for a fight at all."

"You know I can hardly get time off at work."

"You're right, I'm sorry, I shouldn't have implied otherwise," Claudia said.

There was silence on the other end of the phone.

"I'm in the middle of something so if there isn't anything else," Claudia stated.

"Too busy to talk to your big sis for a change?"

This time Claudia folded her arms. "What would you like to discuss?"

"Has mom been taking her pills?"

"That's what you want to talk about?"

"It's just a question."

Claudia had the feeling that Desiree had something on her mind but wasn't in a rush to spit it out.

"Whenever I'm there to shove them down her throat. On the other hand, no."

"Well, when aren't you there?"

"Hmmm," Claudia put a finger to her lip. "How about when I'm at work, or at the grocery store or doing something else adults do."

"Or busy out on a date," Desiree stated matter of fact.

Claudia closed her eyes and sighed, here we go, she thought. "What exactly are you implying, Desiree? Just come on and get it out of your system because we both know this isn't a friendly call."

"I'm just merely saying. I called the house last night and mom told me you were on a date."

"So what, I don't get to date?"

"If you want to be frivolous, you should hire someone to take care of mom while you're doing, whatever it is that you do."

Claudia was on boil. "You have some nerve." Claudia glanced at the man standing patiently waiting for her. She pulled the phone from her ear and silently apologized.

"I'm sorry," she whispered, "I need to take this phone call, so I'll have to come back another time." Claudia pulled a business card from her wallet and handed it to the man. "If you could send me a quote for the dates we spoke about via email that would be great."

"No problem, I'll be in touch, Mrs. Stevens."

Claudia didn't bother to correct him on his salutation, opting to leave the building before the man decided not to rent her anything once her conversation with Desiree got out of control. Stepping through the double doors to the sidewalk Claudia slid the phone back to her ear.

"Look, if you have a problem with the way I'm taking care of mom, you're more than welcome to come over here and do it yourself. I'm sure you have all the time in the world since you have no man, no life, and no business." The words were meant to sting, and they had their intended effect.

"Oh wait, that's right, you can't take an hour lunch break because of your demanding job let alone look after your mother. You can't even make a trip to see her less than every six months." Claudia held her hand out and began a slow clap. "Congratulations, smart ass, you played yourself."

And with that Claudia disconnected the call. She paced back and forth in front of the building before deciding to cross the street to her Toyota. If it was one thing Desiree could do well, it was get up underneath her skin.

By the time Claudia made it back to the car her phone was ringing again.

"What!" she snapped.

The caller hesitated before speaking. "Am I catching you at a bad time?"

All the rage Claudia was feeling dissipated instantly at the sound of Jaden's voice. Her eyes closed and she sighed. "I'm sorry Jaden, I didn't even bother looking at the screen before I answered."

"Then I can be relieved that your vicious tone wasn't meant for me?"

"Of course not, I'm sorry, it's my sister."

"Would you like to talk about it?"

The more he spoke, the more her anger subsided.

"Not really."

"I would like to see you if that's possible."

Her line beeped, and sure enough, it was Desiree. A wave of anger returned. "I'm sorry Jaden, I need to call you back."

"Do what you have to do, chérie."

"You know what," Claudia said. "On second thought, is it okay if I come to you?"

Chapter Nine

Pulling up in front of a massive iron gate, Claudia's Toyota hummed to a stop. She cursed. If her car broke down in front of Jaden's home, she would be mortified. Rolling her window down Claudia reached for the buzzer, but the gate opened before her hand landed on the button. As she waited for the doors to completely open, she said a silent prayer for her Toyota to live until she had the decency to make her getaway.

Claudia hit the pedal, and the Toyota drove into the circular driveway. Not without a sputter or two.

"Come on, Betsy. Please don't fail me now," she whispered to the vehicle.

Claudia cut the engine, and the car shook as it shut down. She closed her eyes briefly and exhaled. This was not the time for her car to start acting up. With everything she was trying to do with the benefit and continuing to grow her business, she couldn't afford to buy a new car. Claudia climbed out and strutted up the four steps to the tall white doors. They opened, and Jaden stood before her with an apron around his muscular waist and a thin white sleeveless t-shirt. Claudia's eyes didn't hide the satisfactory perusal as her vision traveled over his toned arms and what she knew to be a chiseled chest underneath.

The rise of her eyes took in his strong neck and solid jawline, succulent lips, and black lashes, thick and curled upward to perfection. His gaze tormented Claudia, and she was barely able to pull her eyes away. Jaden's layer of chocolate brown skin gave Claudia the impression that he'd been created with thoughts of a candy factory in mind.

"Welcome," he said, his mouth widening into a extensive grin.

Claudia hadn't come over here to have sex with Jaden in the middle of the day. As a matter of fact, her mind was nowhere near that arena when she made the decision to come over. But this man had managed to rid her of the anxiety she experienced minutes before. Hell, maybe he was exactly what she needed in the middle of the day. With the lurid thoughts rambling around her head, Jaden reached out to her, clasping her hand in his.

"Come in, chérie."

She didn't respond, only did what he asked. Jaden led her down an extended hallway past several rooms before they traipsed into a large kitchen. Norma, the family's housekeeper stood in front of the counter with her hands covered in a batch of what seemed to be white flour.

"You remember, Norma, right?"

Claudia found her voice. "I do, from the dinner earlier this year."

During the time Samiyah and Jonas were dating, they were both invited over to Christopher Lee Rose's house for dinner where Claudia and Samiyah met Norma, the family's long-time housekeeper.

"Hello again, Ms. Stevens."

"Hello, how are you?" Claudia spoke.

"I'm fine, thanks for asking. I would shake your hand or even give you a hug, but this one over here has me covered in batter."

"I see," Claudia glanced to Jaden then back to Norma. "What is it that you're making?"

"Well," Norma said, "We're baking fresh cinnamon rolls, pastry muffins, and chocolate chip cookies for the kids at the Boys and Girls Club."

Claudia's eyebrow rose. "Is that right? Smells so good in here. How did this come about?"

"Jonas is a mentor at the club. Has been for years," Jaden said, "But while he's away on his honeymoon, I've stepped in for him. I think the boys like me best anyway." A sexy smile strutted across his lips.

Claudia returned his smile. "I'm sure they do, with you bringing those baked sweets and all."

Norma and Jaden chuckled.

"That's not the only reason."

"You don't have to defend yourself to me. I can see how it's easy to become smitten by you."

Jaden's eyes never left Claudia as she spoke. He still held her hand in his. Jaden moved to stand before her, blocking Claudia's line of sight to Norma.

"Why is that, Claudia? Are you smitten with me?" Jaden bit down on his lip, and his dark lashes lowered, piercing her with a savage glower.

Claudia's voice came out sultry when she spoke. "Maybe. That's for me to know and you to find out."

A dazzling smile curved up her lips. Jaden's gaze dropped down to them. He'd lain awake every night since their trip from Puerto Rico thinking about the lush, soft, fullness of them. Last night's kiss was even hotter than before, and Jaden wanted to know if the next would be just as scorching.

He could get used to sucking her wet mouth in his and Jaden was willing to take every opportunity he had to feel them. It was ironic that he would make a silent vow, not to sexually have her again until the time was right. Jaden had given her the wrong impression, and he would surely rectify that.

Standing in front of her now, even with Norma behind them, didn't keep Jaden from closing the small gap and getting right in her face. Claudia held her breath, and her hands slid up his chest.

"Whatever it is you're thinking of doing to me," she whispered in a purr seeing the savage gleam in his eyes. "You might want to wait until there isn't an audience."

A devilish smile spread across his face, and Jaden held back his words. His eyes traveled from Claudia's layered mane to her dark brown eyes and full lips. It had taken everything in him not to pull her straight to his master bedroom when he'd opened the door and got a look at her pencil suit attire. His eyes had taken in her bodacious curves, and he'd had a flashback.

Once they'd made it to his hotel room back in Puerto Rico, Jaden had been slow with Claudia. Steady. Her body shook under his touch.

"Is everything okay, chérie," he'd spoken, in a voice so thick it had made her body tremble.

"I'm fine."

His hand moved down her shoulder in a sensual caress.

"Are you certain?"

"I am."

Their eyes had locked in a depth of passion. Then Jaden slid his palms down Claudia's hips around to her backside and lifted her by the plumpness of her ass. Claudia's legs wrapped around Jaden's waist; her arms coiling around his neck. The erection that strained against his pants was packed with force as it pushed against her mound. Claudia moaned.

Jaden's lips were on her neck, laying soft kisses as he walked with her over to the bed. While he wanted to take his time, the need to savage her ran thick through him. But he'd savored Claudia, and she'd sang his name throughout the night. Now looking at her, the need to finish what they started was tearing at him every night she was absent from his bed. Coming out of his musing, Jaden laid a light squeeze on Claudia's fingertips.

With trepidation, Jaden switched his focus. "You were having a rough day, something about your sister. Tell me what's going on with you two."

Claudia appreciated the way Jaden changed the subject. She was a second away from dragging him to whatever room lay after this one to feel him pumping inside of her again. As long as they were getting to know each other, she should have her fill of him, right? But how would she ever let a man like Jaden go? The question circled her thoughts on more than one occasion, and Claudia didn't know how to feel about it.

Surely, she could have a platonic relationship with a man. Claudia had many in the past, but Jaden was different. The groove they held together kept a light burning at her center. When it was time to stoke that flame, Claudia wondered if that would be possible.

Shit, she thought. Getting herself worked up about the 'what if's' would certainly drive her mad.

"Let's not ruin the tranquility you've bestowed upon me by talking about my sister."

Jaden arched a brow, a half grin making an appearance. "That I've bestowed upon you?"

Claudia smirked and turned her chin up. "Yeah, you."

Something like a low animalistic growl crawled through him. Claudia's belly was flopping all over the place. She needed a distraction, taking a deep breath, Claudia side stepped him. "Do you need some help, Ms. Norma?"

"If you don't mind getting your hands dirty. Do you have work or can we make a day of it?"

Claudia glanced back at Jaden. "I think I could spare a day."

Jaden folded his brawny arms unable to tear his gaze away from her. As Claudia sauntered over to the sink, his eyes traveled down her silken skin hovering around her abundant hips. Claudia washed her hands and strutted to a corner of the room where she kicked off her shoes.

"I hope you don't mind if I get comfortable."

The question was directed at Norma, but Jaden responded, "Never."

Claudia was fighting like hell to keep her focus on Norma. Being around Jaden kept her unbalanced. She was still trying to figure out how to keep the flutter in her chest from going wild when in his presence.

Norma smirked. "Get as comfortable as you like, Ms. Stevens."

"Norma, you should call me Claudia. There's no need for the formal address."

"If you wish."

Jaden moved across the room headed for the sink. As he washed his hands, Norma spoke to Claudia. "If you'd like to mix this batter right here, I can check on the cookies in the oven."

"These smell so good," Claudia said pulling the sweetly scented bowl across the island to her. "You have no idea how much better my day just became."

Jaden turned off the faucet, bringing an air of heat with him as he crowded her space.

He pulled an empty tray from the counter and sat it in front of him, layering sections of a crème filled dough on the sheet.

"I've decided to start my own nonprofit, Caregivers Organization. I'm in the beginning stages of creating a fundraising benefit for it. I was taking a look at Morgan's on Fulton when Desiree called," Claudia announced.

"That sounds like a lovely nonprofit," Norma chimed. "If you ask me, caregivers don't get enough recognition."

"That's true, but my organization is more focused on being a resource for caregivers in the city of Chicago, than in recognizing them for their efforts. However, now that you mention it, there should be some sort of awards ceremony for them."

"Maybe you could add it to what I'm sure is a long list of duties."

Claudia smiled. "Yeah it's worth it though." She peered over at Jaden who hadn't spoken a word. His penetrating gaze seeming to go on forever. Flustered, Claudia set her focus back on the task she'd been assigned.

"Are you doing this alone?" Jaden finally asserted.

"Yes, I am. Why, do you want to help me?"

"I'd love to help. I've got a few contacts. I'm sure I could pull their attention to the matter."

"When?" Norma asked. "Before or after you finish gawking at her from across the table?"

Claudia choked back a laugh and Jaden turned his mischievous grin on Norma.

"After," he said.

More giggles left Claudia. "Oh you find that funny," his dark voice beat. Jaden grabbed the tray and took it to the oven, sliding it in next to the cookies. He shut the oven door and strolled over to Claudia, wrapping his arms around her from behind.

She laughed, bending and twisting trying to escape his grasp.

"Oh my God, let me go," she laughed, but he didn't. Even Norma was tickled. She'd never seen Jaden this taken with any young lady and Norma had a growing suspicion that their friendship was more than they let on.

"That's enough you two." Norma slung a hand towel at them. "At this rate, the boys will be getting these treats in a few days instead of later today."

"So true!" Claudia chimed in, still caught in Jaden's embrace. "Unhand me, man!" Jaden tickled her more for good measure, and Claudia wiggled, desperate to escape him. Once his fingers had calmed, Claudia was able to regain her composure. Jaden's masculine arms squeezed her, and he brought his lips down on her shoulder in a tender, sweet kiss.

"You know the harder you laugh, the deeper your dimples become."

Claudia blushed. "I hardly pay them any attention anymore."

"I wonder why that is? They're beautiful." He placed a kiss on her cheek absentmindedly, and Claudia blushed again.

Norma cleared her throat, and Jaden held his hands up in surrender. "I'm sorry, mademoiselle," he said to her. "Maybe we should put Claudia out, she's interrupted me." The mirth in his gaze had Norma chuckling now.

Claudia gasped. "Hey, I'll have you know, I'm over here doing what was asked of me. You, sir, are the distraction."

Norma pointed at them both. "If my opinion is anything to the both of you, then I'd say you're collectively a distraction. Even I'm wasting time chastising you two. Why don't you go on a date or something? You've obviously got a thing for one another."

"We've been on a date," Jaden said.

"Well, maybe you should go wherever it is you young folks go after dating for a while."

Instantly, Claudia had a vision of Jaden standing at the altar with an Armani suit tailored to his muscular frame. Just as quickly, she shook the thoughts.

"What do you think, Claudia?"

"Hmm? About what?"

"Would you like to accompany me on a trip?"

Claudia's mind whirled. "Um," she stuttered flabbergasted. "I suppose it's possible. I'd have to check with my sister to see if she has time to look after my mother. Where would we be going?"

Jaden rubbed his chin. "I'm thinking some place fun where we can let loose and play on the wild side."

Claudia's belly flopped. "The wild side?" It was the one thing she was trying to elude. Didn't her mom and sister already think she was irresponsible? However, the term took on new meaning with Jaden. And if the dangerous gaze in his eyes was any indication of that, she was ready to be as foolish with him as foolish could be. You only live once, right?

"There's only one place I know of like that," Claudia spoke.

"I'm listening."

"Vegas, baby."

Chapter Ten

Over the next four hours, Jaden, Claudia, and Norma had officially completed their baking. They worked around the kitchen while chatting about a last-minute trip to Las Vegas, Nevada.

"Have you ever been before?" Jaden had asked.

"Once, in college."

"I assumed you had a good time with your girls?"

"Who said I went with girls?"

Jaden peered at her. "Did you?"

Claudia smirked unable to hold back on him. "Yeah, Samiyah and I went with two other girls from our dorm."

Jaden perked back up. The thought of Claudia in Vegas with a man, boyfriend or not, didn't sit well with him.

"So that means I'll have to make it the time of your life to outdo your girls."

Claudia thought back to her time in Vegas. She gambled 1200 dollars and won 535. They'd found themselves at clubs partying past the midnight hour. Coming out of her thoughts she chimed, "You've got a task on your hands if you plan on outdoing our girl's trip."

"Oh, I'm sure, but trust me, I think I can handle the job."

His voice sent an effervesce of heat trailing down her neck. It nestled between her breasts and her nipples instantly hardened. Rattled, Claudia moved toward the containers to add more sweets to the already growing pile. They all crawled into Jaden's Jeep and pulled up in front of the Boys and Girls Club as soon as the evening school buses arrived to let the children off.

"Jaden!" One of the kids yelled running toward him.

"Hey Zander, how's school?"

Zander rolled his eyes and puffed. "My teacher tells me I should focus in class. She says I wonder off in space a lot, whatever that means."

Jaden smirked. "It means you're not paying attention. Why is that?"

"She talks a lot. Sometimes it's hard for me to keep up and I lose interest."

"Hmmm, tell your mom to come see me before you leave."

"Okay," Zander said. "Did you bring us some sweets, today?" His eyes lit up, hopeful.

This brought on a full smile from Jaden. "Sure did. Now, who's your favorite brother?"

"You are!" Zander sang.

Jaden looked to Claudia. "See, I'm his favorite."

Claudia shook her head. *You're my favorite too,* she thought.

It was 8 pm. when Claudia, Jaden, and Norma arrived back at his home. Jaden pulled into the driveway parking the Jeep behind Claudia's Toyota. He leaned back to Norma.

"You can stay the night, Norma. Don't drive back across town tonight."

"Oh hush, I'll be okay. Besides, you two could use some alone time."

No, Claudia thought. That's exactly what we didn't need lest I turn into an animal and ravage this sexy ass hot-blooded man. The words tickled Claudia causing her to chuckle.

"Norma, have you seen the size of this house? I'm sure we can disappear somewhere inside," he said laying a heavy eye on Claudia.

"I actually should get going myself, or I'll be spending the night, also," she joked.

Jaden's gaze burned through hers. "That can be arranged."

The two watched each other for a long moment. "I can't stay, unfortunately, my mom's home alone."

"She doesn't have to be. Like I said before, that can be arranged." He gave her a lopsided grin. "You never know, she may like it over here and never want to leave."

Claudia's chest was doing something funny to her now. What exactly was he implying? Claudia cleared her throat. "Are you suggesting we go over to my house and pick up my mother?"

"And bring her back here. I'll cook her dinner; she'll relax, get comfortable and never want to leave."

Claudia exhaled a deep breath. "Sounds like you've got it all figured out."

"I can be pretty resourceful you know." Jaden offered her a charming smile. "Besides, she wants to meet me, right?"

"I don't mean to interrupt this chatter, but I'll be going, Mr. Rose."

Jaden cocked a brow at Norma. "Since when do you call me, Mr. Rose?

Norma pursed her lips. "Don't start; you sound like your father."

Norma opened her door, and Jaden jumped out moving swiftly to offer her a helping hand.

"Thank you," Norma said.

Jaden folded his arm through Norma's, and they strolled to her Ford Explorer. Opening the driver side door, Jaden helped Norma into her car. Once she'd gotten comfortable in the seat, he reached over and buckled her belt.

Norma rolled her eyes. "Mr. Rose, I'm capable of buckling my seatbelt. I've been taking care of you and your siblings since you were all in diapers, I think I can manage a seatbelt."

Jaden chuckled, knowing no matter how he responded it wouldn't make a difference. "Doesn't matter, we're old enough to take care of you now." He placed a soft kiss on her forehead. "Drive safely and call me once you arrive at home."

"Yes sir, Mr. Rose."

Jaden threw her a glare and Norma covered her mouth and laughed. Jaden stepped back and closed the door watching as Norma pulled off.

"She adores you, you know."

Jaden rotated around to Claudia reaching out to pull her in by her waist. "I want you to stay." With his lips, Jaden's kiss traveled across her forehead one after the other. Claudia closed her eyes and exhaled, reveling in his caresses.

"I want you to stay," he whispered again between kisses.

Claudia wanted to stay, too, but her obligations wouldn't allow her the satisfaction. As if he'd read her thoughts, Jaden pulled back to look at her. "Your mother can stay as well. We'll take care of her."

Claudia's heart fluttered and confusion set in.

"Why?" She watched him inquisitively.

"You know why."

Claudia thought back to the night in Puerto Rico. She couldn't deny their instant connection, but Claudia didn't believe that they'd get so close that she'd have a hard time moving on when someone else found his interest. Already, the emotions that warmed and rippled through her whenever they were together was frightening

91

enough. It was a bad idea. She couldn't. In the end, it would be a disaster.

But still, she relented. "I'll tell you what, let's go see what she says. My mother's mood swings can be hot and cold sometimes. So, it really just depends on if she wants to be bothered."

Jaden laughed. "She'll want to be bothered."

Claudia arched a brow. "How can you be so sure?"

"She'll be happy to meet me."

Claudia couldn't deny that.

"Come on."

Jaden slipped his arm around her shoulders and walked back to the car. As he held her door open, Claudia climbed inside and Jaden wondered about his intentions. The more he tried to convince himself he was unsure about his actions, the more his actions showed otherwise. Climbing in behind the wheel, Jaden's gaze went to hers, and they both buckled their seat belts synchronously.

He reached out and touched her earlobe pulling a slight tug on it. Claudia blushed feeling like a teenage school girl. Whenever Jaden touched her or said something incredibly sexy, Claudia blushed. Never before had anyone made her feel that way, but Jaden's charm was irresistible. The Jeep reversed and pulled out of the driveway onto the street. Claudia reached for the radio dial and turned it on.

The cruise was relaxing, with the soft tunes reverberating throughout the vehicle. Claudia got comfortable, kicking off her heels pulling her feet into the seat. Jaden rested his forearm on the armrest and Claudia did, too. Their fingers brushed over one another sending currents of warmth stirring through their palms and trickling down their arms. Their eyes connected and they both leaned in.

In a breathy voice, Claudia spoke. "You should probably keep your eyes on the road."

Jaden's attention was everywhere but the road. Claudia's eyes, nose, and lips were becoming his favorite assets on her.

"I've got this."

Jaden's fingers danced along hers. "I wouldn't put you in any danger. Have faith in me."

Claudia's heartbeat was racing again. Jaden took his eyes back to the road and turned the steering wheel. She watched the smooth way he handled the jeep and remembered how he'd taken his time with her in Puerto Rico. A thump in her panties caused her to twist.

Jaden met her gaze again.

Claudia smiled. "I do."

"I do, too," he said. "I mean, have faith in you."

Claudia's smiled lingered. "Of course, what else would you mean?"

Jaden clasped his big masculine hands around hers and pulled it to his mouth for a kiss that scorched her skin and sent a blaze straight through her core. *Shit*, Claudia thought. Who was she kidding? There was no way she could just move on from dating a man like Jaden to any of these other trifling men. What was she going to do? They pulled into her driveway and Claudia watched him quizzically.

"Um, how do you know I live here?"

Jaden put the car in park. "I hope you don't find this creepy but I followed you home last night. After our run in with paparazzi, I needed to make sure you got home safely."

"Why didn't you just tell me, I wouldn't have objected."

Jaden smiled. "I didn't want to distract you further."

That wasn't entirely true, and Jaden knew it. Although he wanted Claudia to get home and check on her mother, Jaden also pondered on the invitation she'd given him. Going back and forth with himself about breaking his commitment to abstain being sexual with her.

But Jaden had won out deciding to keep his distance. It was imperative that he reminded himself of this daily. It was no easy feat hanging around Claudia with the craving that ripped through him anytime he was with her.

Jaden opened his door, and so did Claudia. He followed her up the steps through the front.

"Ma!"

The house was relatively quiet. Claudia strolled down the hallway and turned toward the bathroom.

"Oh my God!"

She darted inside the vestibule. Jaden trotted down the hallway. Claudia had sunk to her knees.

"Mom!"

Claudia shook Adeline who lay naked on the floorboard unmoving. Jaden ran to the room behind him and came back with a blanket that he wrapped around Adeline's body. Steadfast, Jaden lifted Adeline from the floor and took quick strides back down the hallway. Claudia ran after him as they fled the house. She scurried to the back door and opened it jumping inside. Jaden laid Adeline across the seat, her head falling into Claudia's lap. Shutting the door quickly, Jaden made haste pulling out of the driveway to head to Mercy Hospital and Medical Center.

The .22-inch tires burned, coughing up asphalt as Jaden cleared through the streets making sharp turns at every corner.

"Mom, please wake up. Oh my God," Claudia was frantic. She felt Adeline's face. Adeline was warm but her pulse was light. "Oh my God! How could I let this happen?"

Jaden's eyes pulled up to the mirror, catching her reflection.

"Tell me, how much good will blaming yourself do," he said.

Claudia shut her eyes tight as tears streamed down the corners of them.

"I need to call my sister."

Jaden whipped the vehicle into the hospital, parking beneath the underpass. He hopped out pulling open the back door to retrieve Adeline. They ran into the E.R., and Claudia yelled, "Please help us!"

The receptionist hit a button, and a set of double doors opened. Seconds later, doctors and nurses ran out with a stretcher and Jaden laid Adeline down on top of it. The emergency team immediately went about the task of checking her pulse and temperatures as they rushed Adeline inside. On their heels, Claudia and Jaden followed the crew as a doctor threw questions at her one after the other.

"What happened?"

Claudia tossed her arms up letting her hands rest on her head, "I don't know! I wasn't there, I..."

Jaden pulled her into his arms. "We'd just arrived when we found her in the bathroom on the floor. It looks like she may have slipped and taken a hard fall," he finalized.

Claudia's tears increased, and she buckled, but Jaden held her firmly against his broad chest. The team turned into a room, and the doctor put his hand up.

"Stay here please, we'll take care of her. What's your mother's name?"

"Adeline," Jaden responded for her.

"We'll take care of Adeline. Her skin is warm to the touch, so if she's taken a fall, it may just be a need to wake her and get her hydrated. There's a waiting room back around the corner. You should get some water yourself. The doctor patted Claudia on her back and dashed into the room with the other staff.

Claudia cried, and Jaden took an affectionate hand down her back. Her face was nuzzled in his chest as tears spilled down her cheeks.

"Come with me," he whispered, guiding Claudia to the waiting room. At the water cooler, Jaden reached for a plastic cup and filled it halfway. "Take a sip."

Claudia nuzzled her face further into his chest, refusing the cup.

"Chérie," he crooned, "just take a sip, for me."

Slowly, Claudia pulled her face away turning toward the cup. She exhaled deeply and took the cup tossing back the water. As she swallowed more tears sprang from her eyes.

Jaden folded her back into his embrace. It bothered him that she was in so much pain. If he could block her of any hurt or agony, he most certainly would. Claudia rested there allowing him to soothe her. After a minute, she braced her hands against his chest and pulled back. "I need to grab my phone from the car."

"Do you know your sisters number by heart?"

Claudia nodded with somber eyes.

"There's a phone on the wall over there."

"Will it dial long distance?"

"I'm not sure; tell you what, I'll run to the car and get our phones. Are you going to be okay while I'm away?" His deep voice sent shivers through her even now when she was worried for her mother.

"Yes." Claudia moved to sit down on the edge of one the waiting room chairs. Jaden reached for a Kleenex that stretched out of a recyclable box on the table and handed it to her.

"Thank you."

"You're more than welcome."

Jaden lingered a moment longer wondering if the phone call to her sister could wait. Claudia was noticeably anxious to make the call, and he knew their relationship was strained already. Calling her sister would just make it that much worse. On the other hand, Desiree deserved to know her mom was in the hospital.

Claudia glanced up at him. "I'm all right."

"You're not fine, but I'll be back in a flash."

Jaden disappeared around the corner and Claudia sunk into the chair. Placing the Kleenex against her nose she blew into it and discarded the tissue. Saying a silent prayer was all she could do. God and Adeline had a good relationship so talking to him was her best bet. After what seemed like twenty seconds, Jaden reappeared with her phone and purse in hand.

"That was fast," she said.

Jaden sank to a crouch in front of her. He swiped a hand over her smooth, flawless skin and tugged her earlobe. "Can this call wait?"

Claudia watched him for a moment knowing why he asked. She gave him a small smile. "Unfortunately, no."

Dialing the long-distance number Claudia braced herself for the fight that was sure to ensue.

Chapter Eleven

"What do you mean she fell?" Desiree wiped spilled coffee from her blouse as she headed towards the airport while checking when the next flight would fly out. Claudia had called instructing her to drop everything, and now her fingers moved wildly across her screen for the last-minute information. A flight from Houston to Chicago was boarding in twenty minutes, and she had a fifteen-minute ride across the interstate to get there.

"I found her on the bathroom floor. We're at Mercy Hospital and Medical Center, are you leaving now?"

Desiree let out an exasperated sigh. "Yes, I'm on my way." Desiree snapped the phone shut disconnecting the line. To say she was annoyed was an understatement. What had Claudia been too busy doing now that she couldn't be home with their mother?

Desiree's thoughts tornadoed. Was she unreasonable to think it? If Claudia was going to take on the role as a caregiver, she had to put their mother first. This is what Desiree needed to communicate to Claudia. What if Desiree had been at work and not getting off early. What if their mother didn't wake up? The thoughts tormented Desiree, constricting her heart in a way that almost made her lose her breath. Desiree's Ford Focus shot down the highway coming upon its exit. Her thoughts were heavy with words she and her sister would have.

"She hung up on me," Claudia said sitting the phone down.

"You don't seem surprised," Jaden replied.

"Why would I be? It's not like I don't know she hates my guts."

"I'm sure that's not true."

Claudia squinted her eyes. "You want to put some money on it."

"You and Desiree need to have a conversation. From my observation, you both seem like one doesn't understand the other. Just give it a try and see how it goes. At least you'll be able to say; you gave it a shot."

Jaden was right, but Claudia still wasn't feeling it, and she wanted him to go on somewhere with all his good advice. Claudia cracked a small smile at that thought and sighed.

The doctor she'd spoken to on the way in the hospital entered the room.

"Stevens family," he asked.

Claudia rushed to her feet with Jaden right beside her, his hand on the small of her back.

The doctor gave a reassuring smile. "Ms. Stevens is going to be just fine. It turns out it was indeed a hard fall. That's not to say she won't have pain; she will.

There's also a growing lump on her head, but that is to be expected. We'll keep her overnight for observation, and she'll be discharged first thing in the morning."

"Oh my God," Claudia said covering her heart with a hand. "That is such good news, doctor, thank you so much."

Jaden reached out taking the doctor's hand in his for a firm shake. "Thank you, doctor." His arm slid back around Claudia's shoulder.

"Can we see her," Claudia asked.

"Sure, follow me."

They left the waiting room in a different direction than they'd come. It appeared the staff had already taken Adeline to a room on the hospital floor for her overnight stay.

"It's room 2107 to the left," the doctor informed them. "We'll need you to fill out some information so we can get her properly in our systems."

"No problem."

"Do you have everything you need?" Jaden asked turning to Claudia.

"Yes, I keep her insurance information in my purse. Are you leaving now?"

"Not a chance."

Claudia leaned into him. "Thank you for being here. I know it's not an obligation—"

"Sssh," Jaden put his finger to her moist lips. "It is for me," he said.

"Thanks."

"After you."

Claudia walked into the hospital room. Adeline sat upright on the bed with pillows stuffed behind her back. She was awake and her face perked up upon seeing her daughter.

"Hey baby," Adeline said reaching out for a hug.

"Claudia flew into her arms squeezing her snugly.

"I'm so sorry, mama. I should've been there. I don't have an excuse."

"Calm down, calm down," she soothed. "Everything's alright, I just had a little slip and fall."

"A little slip and fall? Mama, you were unconscious on the floor when we found you."

"I'm sorry. I know that scared you to death, but I'm glad you weren't alone." Adeline peered over at Jaden who stood firmly next to Claudia with an affectionate hand on her back.

"Mom this is Jaden, Jaden this is my mother, Adeline."

"It's nice to meet you; not necessarily under these circumstances but nevertheless." Jaden shook her hand.

"Are you the one that keeps my daughter out after hours?"

"Ma!"

"What, I mean after 8 o'clock when I say after hours," Adeline chuckled. "You know for us old folks when the street lights come on, you're late."

Jaden chuckled and Claudia slapped a hand against her head.

"You know it's true," Adeline said to Claudia.

"Ma, if he wasn't the guy, then what? You would've embarrassed me."

"But he is the guy, isn't he?"

A small smile surfaced and Claudia shook her head. "Yes, ma," Claudia gazed back at him, "he is the guy."

Jaden was still stuck on the words Claudia had used. What if he wasn't the guy? Who else is there? Jaden made a mental note to ask her this later. He was suddenly feeling possessive and the thought of Claudia spending time with another man didn't sit well with him.

Adeline glanced back to Claudia. "How did you get me off the floor? I know I weigh a ton."

"You most certainly do not," Jaden spoke up.

Adeline arched an inquisitive brow. "And you would know this because?"

"He's the one that got you to the hospital, ma. We'd still be in the bathroom waiting for an ambulance if I had to bring you myself."

Adeline's eyes roamed over Jaden's muscular physique. The white t-shirt and blue denim jeans he wore sat comfortably against his toned waist. Claudia watched as her mom's eyes rode up and down him again before her cheeks reddened.

"Mom," she whispered.

"What?"

"You're staring."

"Well excuse me, but it's not every day an old lady like me gets swept up in arms like those."

Claudia was horrified, and her eyes popped as her mouth dropped. Jaden chuckled.

"If I need to pass out more often to be in those arms again I just might." Adeline fell against her sheets pretending to fall out. Jaden's chuckle turned into an all-out roar, and Claudia gasped covering her mouth. She couldn't help it though. After several seconds of her mother continuing to lay there, Claudia found her laughter. She shook her head.

"Oh my goodness, I can't even believe you right now."

Adeline opened an eye at them then closed it as if they hadn't seen her. Jaden moved to the other side of Adeline's hospital bed and circled his manly arms around her. A smile surfaced on Adeline's face, and she opened an eye again to peek over at Claudia sticking her tongue out. Claudia continued to laugh, and Jaden was happy that Claudia was back to her calm self.

"They're keeping you overnight, Ma," Claudia said, getting serious.

"I know."

Jaden rose from his position.

"I keep telling them I'm fine. So I knocked myself out, big deal! I have a hard head. I'm okay."

Claudia reached to rub Adeline's forehead. "I'm sorry I wasn't there. I will be next time."

"Is he going to be there, too?"

"Mama, Jaden has a business to run. He can't be around as much as you'd like."

"I can adjust my schedule," Jaden offered.

Claudia stared at him in shocked silence.

"See," Adeline said. "He can adjust his schedule." Adeline perked up even more.

Enough

Claudia didn't know how to feel about what was happening. Was this getting out of hand? What should she make of this?

"Are you hungry, Ms. Stevens?"

"I could use a good meal, why, are you buying?"

"Yes, ma'am, I am."

"As long as it's not this hospital food because you know there's no real chef in the kitchen."

Jaden chuckled. "What would you like?"

"I'm fine with something from a burger joint."

"Mama, maybe we should wait until the doctors tell us what your diet should be."

Adeline reared back with a dismayed expression. "Diet!" She screeched. "I'm not on a diet, low salt, okay? That's about it. Now, don't start Claudia. You're messing up my dinner, and this handsome fella hasn't even gotten it for me yet."

"Low salt, anything else, Ms. Stevens?"

Adeline smiled. "Na'll that'll be all. Thanks."

"You're most welcome." Jaden turned his gaze to Claudia. "And you chérie, what would you like?"

"Cherie? Her name is Claudia. Now I don't know what you—"

"Mom!" Claudia almost died. "Chérie is French for sweetheart," she whispered sharply.

Adeline gasped and folded her arms. "Oooh, that's so nice. I'm sorry, I don't' know anything about French. I thought you forgot my baby's name."

Claudia groaned. She could've slid to the floor and hid up under the bed. Jaden couldn't stop laughing, "It's quite alright. Trust me, I understand, but I could never forget Claudia's name. She's not one to easily be forgotten."

His smooth tone sent an undulation of heat through Claudia's nervous system. With their gazes locked, Jaden spoke to Claudia. "What would you like to eat, chérie?"

"I'll take anything you bring back."

"I'll return shortly then." Jaden circled the bed and pulled Claudia into an embrace placing a soft kiss against her temple. He released her and left the room.

Adeline looked to her daughter. "That is one fine ass man." Adeline shook her head slowly. "His daddy still alive?"

Three hours later

Desiree rushed through the double doors of Mercy Hospital and Medical Center emergency room and ran to the front desk.

"I'm looking for my mother, Adeline Stevens. She was rushed here unconscious."

Desiree's nails raked across the desk as she waited impatiently for the nurse to look up the information. Frantic Desiree yelled, "Could you hurry it up!"

The clerk's eyes shot up bewildered. "She's in room 2107. It's through these doors, down the hall to the very end, then to the right."

Desiree shot down the hall, moving past other doctors and nurses coming out of patient's rooms.

"Ma'am you can't run down this hall!" A nurse yelled, but Desiree ignored her and continued her race to 2107. She was almost out of breath when she stumbled upon the room. Entering quickly, Desiree came to a sudden halt at what was before her. Her mother, Adeline, sat perched on the hospital bed with two men; each one on each side giving them goofy grins.

Desiree couldn't get her argument out quick enough when her eyes drifted to their God given form. Both men were dressed casually in jeans and a t-shirt, but the tone in their muscular arms, flat abs, and firm thighs said they were regulars at the gym. Besides that, she'd never seen men so flawlessly beautiful. Creamy smooth skin, one dark brown the other light brown like the sun had barely kissed his skin. Desiree was thinking of ways she could kiss his skin, and her body traitorously yearned for the one on the left. "Jesus," she whispered.

Adeline glanced up with a fork halfway to her mouth.

"Hey baby, come in!" Adeline lit up. The two men looked to Desiree and Desiree knew that God had no doubt created them to perfection. *Damn.*

"Hello," the one on the right said. "I'm Jaden, this is my brother, Julian."

Julian fixed Desiree with a devastatingly handsome gaze and rose to his feet. "Greetings, would you like to sit here next to your mom?"

His voice ricocheted off her ear drums causing the beat in her heart to surge. Desiree went to respond when the bathroom door opened and out walked Claudia. The sisters came face to face for the first time in six months.

"Desiree," Claudia said with an air of surprise in her voice.

"Claudia," Desiree retorted. "You seemed surprised. You did remember I was coming, didn't you?"

Claudia closed the bathroom door. "How could I forget?"

Three pairs of eyes were on them as they both held back what was on their minds in front of their mother. Jaden noticed the change of emotion that ran across Claudia's face and the substantial need to hold her tugged at his spirit.

"Come over and give your mother a hug or are you going to stand there staring at your sister," Adeline spoke to Desiree.

Desiree strutted over to her mom passing Julian on her way. She glanced at him and couldn't help but get a sniff of his all male scent. Her belly rumbled, and Desiree wasn't in need of food. Thrown off her game, she turned from him and threw her arms around Adeline.

"Hey, mama." Desiree caressed the side of Adeline's face. "How are you, I was so worried when Claudia told me you were unconscious."

"Yeah, just a slip and fall. But my handsome hero over here came to my rescue, so I'm fine now." Adeline shrugged like it was nothing.

Desiree's brow raised. "Your handsome hero?"

"Yeah, Jaden," Adeline pointed to him and Jaden smirked waving a hand in Desiree's direction.

"And would you know, he has a brother. Multiple brothers."

Desiree took her gaze back to Julian who was still standing idly beside her. "So he does," Desiree said. She took a hand down her hair, self-consciously checking her appearance. "I guess these are Claudia's friends."

"They're my friends now. I mean... too, they're my friends, too," Adeline corrected. Julian and Jaden held amused smiles.

"Maybe you could get to know Julian better. Claudia's already got dibs on Jaden."

"Mama!" Claudia blushed mortified. Could her mother be more embarrassing? "I don't have dibs on anyone. Oh my God." Claudia tried to wipe the humiliation from her face. "We're going to step out for a minute." Claudia pivoted on her heels clutching Jaden's hand in hers.

"I should probably step out, too," Julian reached over and shook Adeline's hand. "It was nice to meet you, mom." He turned his attention to Desiree. "It was nice to meet you, albeit briefly."

Julian's thick brows strong nose and moist lips sent Desiree's nerves into a frenzy.

"Maybe one day we can become more acquainted." Julian finished.

"Maybe," Desiree heard herself saying.

Julian offered her a charismatic grin that budded her areolas.

"I'll hold you to it." Julian winked and strolled to the door. Desiree and Adeline looked after him. His strut was confident and strong; looked like he had a nice ass too.

Desiree had a brief picture of him thrusting inside her, and she gasped and shut her eyes.

"Honey, I need to meet Christopher," Adeline said.

"Who's Christopher? Another brother?"

"No, their father, chile."

Desiree shook her head. "Mama!"

"What? Shoot, I asked Jaden about him, and he says Christopher is single. Has been for years since their mother's passing. It's a touching story, and I'd be willing to touch Christopher all the way through a retelling of it."

"Mama!"

"What!"

"That is just a little too far! I am your child."

"And how do you think you got here child?"

Desiree scoffed. "Jesus! What will I do with you?"

"You'll love me until you can't no more and get yourself hooked up with that fine man. They own their own businesses. You better snatch that other one up before he's off the market."

"That's not how love works, mama."

"Shit, you'll learn to love each other later."

Desiree giggled and shook my head. "Here I am thinking you've got one foot in the dream world and one foot in the real world and you up in the hospital gawking after gorgeous men."

Adeline wiggled her eyebrows. "It's fantastic, right? I told Jaden I should pass out more often."

Desiree pursed her lips and sauntered off.

"Um excuse me, ma'am, where are you going," Adeline asked.

"To talk to your daughter."

"You mean your sister."

"Yeah, that one."

"Hey," Adeline said.

"Give her a break; she's been doing a good job taking care of me."

"Yeah, looks like she's been doing a fantastic job," Desiree said as she strolled through the door in search of Claudia.

Chapter Twelve

Desiree found Claudia outside against a Jeep Cherokee. "Can I speak to my sister for a minute, please?" Desiree's tone was curt and straight to the point.

Jaden removed his arms. "Julian's getting ready to head overseas for another photo shoot. I'm going to the airport to see him off. Tell me what you need so I can get it for you."

"I don't need anything, and you don't have to come back, Jaden. You've done enough. It's late, you should head home and get some R & R."

"How about, you let me worry about R & R. It's you that's my concern right now."

Claudia smiled. "Text me first."

Jaden leaned in laying an ultrasensitive kiss on Claudia's face, he turned to Desiree and inclined his head. "Have a good night."

Desiree didn't respond; instead, she twisted her lips at Claudia.

"What the actual hell, Claudia."

"Can you wait until he's out of earshot before you jump down my throat please?"

Desiree inhaled and exhaled deeply, and they moved away watching the men crawl into the Jeep. Jaden and Julian waved, smiled, and winked at the women before pulling out of the parking lot.

"So this is what you've been up to," Desiree said flatly.

Claudia inhaled a deep breath. "Listen, Jaden and I are just friends. Nothing more."

Desiree smirked. "Does he know that?"

"What's that supposed to mean?"

"Come on Claudia, Jaden is all over you. I've been here all of thirty minutes and I can tell he has the hots for you." Desiree twisted her lips at the puzzled look on Claudia's face. "You're trying to tell me you honestly don't know?"

"I know he likes me, but I like him, too."

Desiree scrutinized her sister carefully. "Like, huh?"

Claudia folded her arms.

"Look, I don't want to jump down your throat all the time. But you're my kid sister, and I feel like you don't take life seriously sometimes. It's time to grow up Claudia. You're taking care of our mother. Now when do you plan to get your head on straight?"

Claudia's head fell back, and she shut her eyes tight then reopened them and glared at her sister. "You're a liar and a hypocrite."

Desiree was insulted. Her eyes rising in surprise.

"Yes, I said it. Every chance you get to criticize me, you do. I never hear you say, thank you, Claudia for stepping up to take care of our mother. Or, you don't ever call to check on my well-being, see how I'm handling doing all of this alone. I mean for God's sake, Desiree. I co-own a business. I'm trying to plan a fundraiser, and yes, I am lonely. All the time. I would love to have a man like Jaden! But I'm not stupid. I know Jaden could never be with a girl like me. His reputation would probably be ruined! But I can enjoy the time I spend with him, can't I? I can pretend to have some sort of life! Oh no, but as soon as I go and do that something happens, or nothing happens, and I still get criticized!"

Claudia wiped the tears that threatened to fall. "Shit," she groaned. "I don't need this from you, Desiree, since you think you're so perfect. Why don't you do it yourself?"

"I never said I was perfect," Desiree retorted.

"Yeah, you don't have to. Just continue shaming me for everything I don't get right." Claudia moved past Desiree marching into the hospital.

"We're not done!"

"I am!"

"Claudia, let me talk to you!"

But Claudia disappeared into the hospital's entrance.

Over the next few days, Jaden reached out to Claudia but received minimal conversation. He was aware that the stress of her sister being around and Adeline's recent hospitalization had something to do with. He reasoned she was busy, but that didn't stop him from wanting to check on her. In any case, Jaden would give her the space she required, for now. Strolling into Rose Bank and Trust Credit Union, Jaden spoke and nodded to fellow employees. Jaden's presence was announced when his leather oxford shoes tapped against the marble floor. He checked his Rolex and waited patiently for the elevator doors to open.

"Sir," A young intern spoke.

Jaden turned to him. "Good morning, Dominique. How's everything going?

"Going good, sir, I've got the newspaper for you." Dominique handed over the paper with a fresh cup of coffee. "Black no milk, like you prefer it."

Jaden grinned at the enthusiastic intern, eager to please. "Thank you Dominique, but you shouldn't have. We're not paying you as it is. Did you use the company card to make these purchases?"

Dominique shook his head no. "It's just coffee and a newspaper. I've got a little savings."

"Next time use the company card, it's no problem."

"Yes, sir."

The elevator doors dinged, and a group of people exited. Jaden stood to the side until the last one was off then slid into the elevator just as the doors began to close. Arriving at the floor that held his headquarters, Jaden made his way through the office building.

"Mr. Rose," his assistant cooed. "You have a visitor. I didn't see any appointments, but she said it was last minute, so I hope you don't mind me letting her sit inside your office."

Enough

Jaden leaned to look through his office doors opening.

"Next time, give me a call, Samantha and I may have you reschedule. I have a conference call in 30 minutes."

"I'm sorry, sir. I can reschedule an appointment for her now."

"Next time."

Jaden proceeded into his office his confident strides taking him around his desk. He sat the cup of coffee on the mahogany surface, his eyes connecting with his guest.

Sitting with her legs crossed bouncing slightly, Cassie offered Jaden a sensual smile. "Good morning, Mr. Rose."

The fact that his name didn't sound nearly as befitting as it did when Claudia said it was all the more reason for Jaden to want to end this meeting before it started.

"What can I do for you this morning Cassie?"

Her eyes fell to his lips then back to his honey brown eyes.

"I was wondering if you could help me out. I'm offering free dance classes to inner city kids and am in need of a partner. So far, I've got one hundred and fifty kids who've signed up, so I'll be teaching classes throughout the week, sometimes five a day." Cassie shifted in her seat. "I know you're a busy man Mr. Rose—"

"Just call me, Jaden," he offered.

Cassie's brows quirked. "Okay, Jaden. As I was saying, I know you're a busy man, but if you could afford to spend an hour every other day or so, that would help me out." Cassie's smile lit up the room, and she batted her eyes.

Jaden unbuttoned his jacket and pulled his long arms out of it, tossing it over the back of his chair. Cassie's read-through was bold since her gray eyes paused on every part of him before returning to his sexy masculine face. Jaden pondered her request. He was always one to help out inner city kids or any kids, for that matter. But, being in such close proximity with Cassie on a regular basis was not something he looked forward to.

"I would love to help, Cassie, but unfortunately, I'll have to turn you down."

Cassie's smile fell. "Why?" She almost snapped.

Jaden grimaced. "As you said before, I'm busy these days, and I'm sure you can find some other gentleman that would be willing to help you out."

"I'm not sure about that."

"Once you make your offer known, you'll have a line around the corner." Jaden offered her a half a grin. Cassie was feeling more disappointed by the second.

"Not even on weekends?"

Jaden thought more about her request. "I may be able to come through twice a week at most, but I can't guarantee it."

Cassie wasn't completely deflated. She offered Jaden a warm smile.

"I'll take what I can get," she cooed.

When she didn't rise from her seat, Jaden spoke. "I have a conference call in ten minutes, is there anything else?"

"Oh, I'm sorry." Cassie found her feet and moved towards the door. "I was wondering if you'd like to have lunch today." Before Jaden responded she quipped, "A man's gotta eat, right?"

"I'll let you know."

"Great, I'll check in around noon then."

Jaden inclined his head as he watched the animated blonde strut out of his office. Thoughts of Vegas resurfaced. Jaden would rather take Claudia to Morocco, but she'd mentioned Las Vegas before he'd had the chance to offer it. Jaden hit the speaker on his desk phone and dialed Samantha's extension.

"Yes sir," she answered.

"Samantha booked two tickets to Las Vegas, Nevada this weekend, round trip. I'll send you the details in an email."

"Yes sir, I'll look out for it."

"Thank you."

"Oh, Mr. Rose, your nine o'clock is on the phone."

"Send him through, Ms. Davies."

The phone beeped, and Jaden answered, but his thoughts were on Vegas, and the time he would get to spend with Claudia. She was full of excuses these days, but he had an idea that would free her of all her obligations. The sooner he could get to her, the better.

Chapter Thirteen

Samiyah Manhattan strolled into S & M Financial Advisory with a bounce in her step. Humming a little tune that had gotten stuck in her head over her honeymoon vacation, Samiyah sauntered up to Claudia's office only to find it empty.

"Hmm."

Turning away, Samiyah headed for her office and pulled to a stop at the sight of her missing friend.

"I went by your office and wondered where you were," Samiyah spoke.

Claudia twirled the visitor's chair she sat in and smiled up at Samiyah. She held her arms out. "Here I am, waiting for you."

"I see, what up, girl."

"Wow, you're so calm, relaxed and refreshed."

Samiyah smiled demurely. "How can you tell?"

Claudia gawked. "For one, you're glowing. Are you pregnant?"

Samiyah reared back and laughed. "Not that I'm aware of, but hey, who knows after the way my man rocked my whole world. I wouldn't be surprised."

"You lucky, lucky, girl!"

Samiyah laughed. What's up with you and Jaden?"

Claudia sighed. "Girl, I am going through it over here, okay? You being gone on your honeymoon made me hold this ordeal all to myself, even though Octavia and Serena tried to get up in my business."

Samiyah chuckled. "You should've told them. You know they're cool."

"Yeah, but it's not the same as talking to you."

Samiyah nodded. "So, what is it?"

"It's Jaden."

Samiyah pulled her chair out and sat down crossing her legs. She placed her elbows on the desk and rested her chin in her upturned palms.

"I'm listening."

"He's... everything."

"Mmhmm, continue," Samiyah said.

"We've been around each other since we left Puerto Rico, and he's so attentive, and suave, I don't even know how to take him. You know we went dancing. I mean, he took me to a dance studio where he taught me how to tango."

Samiyah's smile became bright, and her eyes twinkled. "Sounds like love to me."

"Girl don't I wish! The way he speaks to me and treats me like I'm the only woman in the world is working overtime on my emotions."

"Sounds like the way Jonas treats me."

"Really?"

"Mmhmm, they are brothers, so yah know."

Claudia sulked in her seat.

"I don't understand your grief," Samiyah continued.

"Samiyah, I can't keep going around acting like this is okay. I'm..." Claudia paused and nibbled on her bottom lip.

"Spit it out girl; you're what pregnant?"

Claudia gasped her mouth falling open. "Girl no!" Claudia moved to Samiyah's office door and shut it quietly.

"Octavia and Serena's doors are closed, they have clients," Samiyah pointed out.

"That's not the point."

"Okay, so tell me what's the problem?"

Claudia trod back to her seat and plopped down. "I'm falling in love with him."

Samiyah's lips curved into an excited grin, but Claudia was shaking her head no. "This is not a good thing."

Samiyah frowned. "Huh, why not?"

"We're talking about a Rose brother! The most elite men in Chicago. We've talked about this. You know what kind of women they're usually seen with."

"And what am I? Chopped liver," Samiyah asked with her arms held out. "I'm nothing like those women, and like you said, we've had this conversation before so why are you worried about it?"

"Because, what if he's just around for a while. You know to have a little fun then be off to the next woman giving him attention. I've had men come and go before, but this is different. I never fell in love with any of them, and frankly, it's not fair for Jaden to do this to me. He knows what kind of allure he has over me." Claudia stuck her lip out. "I'm afraid, Samiyah. I'm scared I'm going to fall for him and he's going to break my heart." Claudia's voice softened. "Then I'll be a wreck, and I don't have time to deal with this kind of thing. You know my mom fell and we had to take her to the hospital and now my sisters down here and—"

"Whoa!" Samiyah said as Claudia rambled on.

With her brows furrowed Claudia said, "What?"

"Slow down just a minute. You can't just ramble all that out without intermission. Back up, first, your mom fell!"

Claudia's shoulders sagged. "Yes, I was with Jaden. We'd spent the day making sweet treats for the kids over at the boys and girls club when we went to check on her. We got there and she was passed out in the middle of the bathroom floor. I freaked out!"

"Oh my God, I'm sure you did. Is everything okay?"

"Yes, she's fine now, and pouting every now and again about all the attention Desiree, and I are showing her at home."

"What was the reason for her falling out?"

"Getting out the shower and just lost her footing, I guess."

"That's why Desiree's in town."

Claudia pursed her lips. "She called me earlier that same day saying she would be down for the weekend. With my mom falling that just pushed her trip ahead. And you know she didn't give me any slack."

Samiyah frowned. "Oh my," she said. "You need a girl's night out, huh?"

"Sho you right."

Samiyah watched her friend for a moment. "Did you tell Jaden you're falling for him?"

"Um, no ma'am. I'm not about to make a fool of myself."

"Then how do you know?"

"Know what?"

"You said, Jaden knows what kind of allure he has over you. How can you be certain of that if you haven't told him?"

Claudia thought about her question. "I'm sure Jaden is well aware of the lure he has over all women."

"Do you really think Jaden would just stop seeing you for no reason and move on to someone else?"

"When he gets bored like most men do, yeah."

"I don't think you believe that. Jaden seems pretty structured to me. From the moment I met him, he's been nothing but open and charismatic."

Claudia bit the inside her jaw thinking about Samiyah's words.

"You're saying this vibe we've got going is real?"

"I don't see why not, but the only way for you to know for sure is to ask. What's the worst that can happen? At least then you'll be clear about his intentions, and if you need to pull back to protect your heart, then do so."

"I've kind of already started."

"What do you mean?"

"I've been dodging his calls, and when I do answer the phone, I keep it short and sweet."

"How do you want this to turn out? I'm asking just for the sake of knowing what you want."

Claudia flipped her heels off with the curve of her feet and pulled them into her chair as she pondered. "I want more. I want to know him in every way, be his shoulder to cry on, love him, mentally, physically, in every way possible."

A small smile appeared on Samiyah's face. "That's what you tell him, sweetie."

"Samiyah, I can't tell him that."

"Why not?"

"I'm a coward. What if that's not what he wants, I'd be crushed. I'd rather just continue to ignore his calls and blow him off to save myself the heartache."

"Then you'll always wonder what if. And whenever you come over to our place you'll possibly be in his company. Can you imagine, Jaden with a girlfriend, wife or confidant other than you?"

The images assaulted Claudia's mind, and her stomach churned. By the look on her face, Samiyah guessed she didn't like that picture at all.

"Exactly," Samiyah said. "But it's inevitably up to you."

Claudia's head fell into her hands, and she groaned.

"Find your courage. I've witnessed you grow since we were teenagers. If anyone deserves their happily ever after, it's you. Don't be discouraged because of what you think can happen. Go for it with everything you've got."

Enough

Chapter Fourteen

When Desiree opened the door to find Jaden on the porch, surprise registered across her face. "Jaden, right," she asked, holding a finger out at him.

"Yes, how are you, Desiree?" His voice dripped with a profound thickness.

"Much better than the last time you saw me. Claudia's not here."

"I'm aware. I would like to speak to you and Ms. Stevens for a moment if at all possible."

"Oh, sure," she widened the door allowing him entrance. "My mom is in the living room, this way."

He followed Desiree to the living room where Adeline sat with her feet propped up on the couch watching soap operas. Upon his entrance, Adeline's face brightened. "Jaden, how are you, son?"

Jaden sauntered to Adeline and bent down to scoop her up in a tight embrace, "I'm doing just fine. How are you, Ms. Stevens?"

"Oh, I'm spectacular. Been having these girls fussing over me ever since that incident." Adeline rolled her eyes, and Jaden chuckled.

"That's what they're supposed to do."

"Yeah, I hear you, but I've had enough. You think you want to be fawned over until it happens. Then suddenly, you have no tolerance for it. Know what I mean?"

"As a matter of fact," Jaden drawled, "I do."

"I'm sure." Adeline swept her legs off the couch and sat up. "What brings you by today? I know you didn't come by just to visit lil ole me."

"I would've checked on you sooner, but it's been hard for me to get in touch with Claudia for more than five minutes. Any idea why that is?"

He glanced from Adeline to Desiree.

"I told that girl to get out of the house. Her last couple of days have consisted of her going back and forth to work. She's also got this fundraiser she wants to put together, but I'm afraid she won't have enough money to fund it unless she pulls from her savings. And she won't do that because she likes to save every penny she has."

"She went to the bank for a loan, ma," Desiree injected. "But other than that, I may have something to do with your short conversations."

Jaden held a firm eye on Desiree. "Why is that," he asked smoothly.

Desiree sighed. "I'm hard on her, I always have been. It's a long story, but I know she likes you a lot and I don't mean to be so intolerable."

"What can you do to fix that, Desiree?"

Jaden's question was more of a statement. He was telling her to do something about it. His bravado made Desiree smirk.

"I'm not sure, I guess lighten up."

"I've got an idea," Jaden's bass-filled voice drummed.

"Yeah?"

"Yes, I want to take Claudia on a trip. If you could hold things down here at the house without troubling her. That would be a start."

"A trip, huh?" Adeline said. "Where are you going?"

"I'll let her tell you when she gets back."

"When are you leaving?" Desiree asked.

"Tonight." Jaden glanced from Adeline to Desiree. "Would that be a problem?"

The two women shrugged. "What about her business?"

Jaden fancied them with a sexy grin. "Let me work out the details, you just do your part." His voice was stern as he watched Desiree. Jaden and his brother's intoxicating stares were enough to make a woman do whatever they wanted. Desiree was sure she hadn't agreed to something so quickly without putting up a fight before. She could see why Claudia was so taken by Jaden and why she'd seemed depressed lately with him not around.

"Well alright," Adeline said. "Have fun and bring me back a souvenir."

"Will do," Jaden rose to his feet. "I'll see myself out."

"No, no!" Claudia swatted her steering wheel. "Come on Betsy don't fail me now!"

The Toyota Camry stuttered, and smoke billowed from the engine. Claudia let out a series of harsh expletives as she pulled the car to the side of the highway. With the steering wheel clutched in both her hands she shook it, and her head fell into the horn. It blared, and she jumped.

"Shit," she swore.

Claudia pulled her cell phone out and went through her contacts. "David, Gerald, Paul," she muttered going through the choices of men that could possibly come and help her. When she came to Jaden's name, she paused with her finger hovering over the call button. Samiyah had given her sound advice, but Claudia was still hesitant on whether to take it. To reveal the way she felt to him was scary in more ways than one.

There was a sharp knock on her window and Claudia jumped as she glanced up.

"Need help?" The stranger asked.

Claudia opened her door and stepped out with her hair swaying with the wind. "Yeah, my engines busted I believe. I just need to call triple A."

The young fare skinned brother smiled and pointed behind her. Claudia glanced around to see a tow truck.

"I'm not triple A, but I think I can get the job done."

Claudia grinned. "Oh my luck is never this good. How much?"

"Fifty."

"You got it, let's go!"

"Grab whatever you need out of your vehicle, and you can sit in mine while I get your Toyota hooked up."

Claudia did take note of the way the man's gaze landed on every part of her. "What did you say your name was again?" she asked.

"Marcus." He held his hand out for a shake. "And you are?"

"Claudia, nice to meet you, Marcus."

"Very nice indeed," Marcus stated.

An hour later, Claudia's Toyota was with her friendly neighborhood mechanic. She'd went to pay Marcus for the tow, but instead of payment, he'd asked for her number. When she declined, he'd given her his. That gave Claudia a chuckle.

"You're not used to taking no for an answer, huh?"

"Not when I'm determined."

"I would rather pay you. I don't want to give you an impression that I'll be calling you."

"Why," he glanced to her ring finger. "Are you married?"

"Um, no."

"Long term relationship?"

"You don't have to keep guessing. I'm single but not looking."

"Unless the right man comes along," he said.

Claudia smirked. "And I guess you're the right man, then?"

Marcus put on a full-blown smile. "I can be."

Claudia gave a rueful grin with a shake of her head.

"The least you could do is tell me how your repairs went. If all else fails, I know a mechanic who could get it done for you at a reasonable price."

Claudia laughed. "Laying it on a bit thick, aren't you?"

"What can I say, I try."

"Thank you for your kindness, Marcus, I think. See yah."

Claudia crawled into the back of her Uber and closed the door. Marcus waved her off and she waved back. She gave out directions to the driver, and he pulled away. When Claudia's phone rang, she checked the screen to see Samiyah's face.

"Hey, I'm on my way home, what's up?"

"Pack a bag and meet me at my place in one hour."

Claudia pursed her lips. "You know I can't just jump up and leave all willy nilly!"

Samiyah chuckled. "I've got it covered. Mom's being taken care of. Just pack a bag like I said, no more questions or concerns. I wouldn't tell you to if I didn't have everything under control."

Claudia wondered what her friend was up to. "See you in an hour," Claudia said.

There was a limousine parked in front of Samiyah and Jonas' three-story brick stucco house. Grabbing her bag and exiting her Uber, Claudia strolled passed the limo when the door opened. Her heart lurched upon seeing Jaden's long, athletic frame pull out to stand before her. He was dressed in a comfortable short sleeve button down that kissed the undertones in his chest. The blue jeans he wore hung just slightly off his hips, and suddenly, Claudia was jealous of the denim material.

Her eyes roamed back to his cinnamon smooth skin, strong jawline, sexy lips and honey brown eyes that held a twinkle of mischief.

"Good evening, chérie."

His dark voice sent a wave of goosebumps threading down her skin. He took an uncalculated step toward her and cuffed her hand in his.

"Follow me."

And she did. God help her, she would follow this man to the moon and back. Sliding inside the limo, Claudia kept her eyes on him as he moved in beside her and tapped the partition. The limo pulled away from the curb and Jaden reached for her hand, sliding his fingers inside hers.

Claudia cleared her throat and found her voice. "I was supposed to meet Samiyah at her house."

Jaden pulled her hand to his lips, the soft moistness of them making her shiver. "You were meeting me," he said. "Since I've been unable to reach you, I thought maybe you would respond better if Samiyah called." His voice was smooth and inviting.

"So, you set me up?"

Jaden pierced her with a feral gaze. "Whatever it takes."

Claudia's heart leaped, and she frantically searched for the power window's button to let in some air.

"Where are we going?"

"Wherever you want to."

"Just like that?"

He inclined his head. "Why are you sitting over there, are you afraid to be near me, Claudia?"

Hell yes, she was, but instead of voicing that expression, she only swallowed and offered him a small smile.

"Of course not." She scooted next to him, and he placed a comfortable arm around her.

"Much better."

Claudia relaxed into Jaden side. She could get used to this. *You should tell him how you feel.* Shaking the thoughts, Claudia made up her mind to enjoy this time. If he went through the trouble of tracking her down to be with her again, then she'd enjoy their time together. When they pulled into the airport, he'd sparked her interest. The chauffeur opened their door, and Claudia grabbed her lone bag and purse. Jaden reached over and took it off her hands.

"It's just one bag; I can carry it no problem," she said.

"I'm sure you can."

Claudia realized he was being a gentleman. "I'm sorry, I'm used to doing things on my own."

"Hmmm, we'll have to do something about that, too."

"Oh yeah, what do you propose?"

Jaden leveled her with a sexy grin. "Punishment."

Claudia's belly flopped. "In that case," she said, "I've been a very bad girl. You should punish me hard, Mr. Rose."

A low rumble bellowed from him, and the strain against his pants was painful. He glanced down then back to her. "Look what you did."

Claudia was looking, and it tickled her fancy that she could discombobulate him just as much as he did her.

"Well," she purred, "We'll just have to do something about that, too. Won't we?"

The dark hunger in his eyes told her that she would pay for being a tease. He took a step forward pinning her against his chest and the limo. For several suffused minutes they stared, drowning in one another. Claudia's breathing was laboring on un-control, and they were merely standing, feeling each other's vibes. Translucent but strong. So potent that if he touched her, she would surely crumble in his arms. But he didn't. Stepping back from her, Jaden took in a heavy breath.

"We should get going, or we'll miss our flight."

Coming out of her trance, Claudia smoothed her hands down her sides in an attempt to regain her emotions.

"You never told me where we were going."

"Vegas."

Claudia gasped pulling back a broad smile. "As in Las Vegas, Nevada?"

"That's the one."

She squealed elated, and he grinned reaching out to pull her into the safety of his chest. They walked, linked arm and arm. The plane ride from Chicago to Las Vegas was a smooth one; no turbulence, and Claudia slept leaning into Jaden for the entire ride. When she woke, the fasten your seatbelt light dinged.

She glanced around and stretched. "We're here already?"

"Yes, chérie, you slept like a baby. Working hard I suppose."

Claudia nodded. "Being at home with Desiree hasn't been the easiest these days. But I don't want to talk about her, we're in Vegas!" she squealed again. "I suppose this trip will be completely different from my all girls trip, but," her voice dipped. "I'm confident it'll be much better."

"Are you now?"

"Yes."

The flight attendant's voice sounded through the speakers as Jaden reached for Claudia's chin with a simple caress.

"I think you may be on to something."

She sucked her lip between her teeth. Jaden's fingers roamed down her neck, and she arched her neck reveling in the simple pleasures of his touch. Her heart raced as he applied pressure, and rubbed an affectionate thumb in a circle on her skin.

Her eyes closed and she purred. "Mmm, Jaden..."

When she reopened them, the desire she saw back at Chicago's airport resurfaced. Jaden was not trying hard enough to keep his hands to himself, and he was paying for it dearly as his libido screamed. Why did he want Claudia so bad? Why was their energy undeniably stimulating? When his hands touched her skin, it sent a blaze coursing through his veins that was mind bending. And having her all to himself for the next three days would prove difficult if he wanted to stay on his mission to show her what they had going on was not only physical. *Damn,* he thought. This was going to be harder than he thought.

Chapter Fifteen

When the door to the Palazzo Hotel opened, Claudia's mouth dropped. She'd stayed at her fair share of luxury hotels, but the upscale opulence of this resort was flawlessly decorated with plush carpet, modern furnishing, and marble bathroom floors.

"This is incredible," she said. "I don't know if I brought enough clothes for this trip." Claudia began to mumble to herself. "Samiyah didn't say how long we'd be staying or anything, just grab a bag we're going on a trip," she mimicked.

Jaden chuckled. "No worries, chérie, we'll go shopping."

Claudia's eyes brightened. When she was in college, her spending was limited on her all girls trip to Vegas. However, now that she co-owned and operated her dream business, Claudia reasoned she had a few thousand she could throw away. She squealed, and Jaden approached her. He laid a warm kiss against her temples.

"I'm going to freshen up, and I'll be back for our shopping extravaganza."

"Wait, where are you going," she asked reaching out for him.

Turning back to her, Jaden slid his hands into his pockets. "To my suite, chérie."

"Oh, so you're not staying here with me?"

Jaden smirked, knowing if he stayed they would not make it out of the hotel room. "This suite is yours; however, I'm only next door in the adjoining room if you need me."

But Claudia didn't want him to leave. She'd been trying to figure out what it was she said that made him pull back from being sexual with her. And it was becoming increasingly difficult for Claudia to abstain from jumping his bones.

"Oh, okay, I guess."

Jaden took her chin in his hand. "Whenever you want me, I'm just a knock away."

Claudia wanted him now, and although she wanted to tell him to stay, she was afraid of what he might say. So instead, she shook her head up and down.

"Okay, I'll freshen up, too."

Jaden leaned in and placed another kiss on her forehead before taking his leave. When the door closed behind him, Claudia fell back on the bed with arms wide. *Oh my God, I can't believe I'm here with this man.* She rolled into the sheets stuffing her face into the fresh linen's fragrance. Her legs swung as she kicked with excitement. *Calm down girl; you act like you've never been out of the city.* But Claudia couldn't calm herself. Her upbringing in the hood of Chicago wasn't a pleasant experience. Sometimes their family would go hungry on days their mother had to pay the rent and electricity.

Now that she had the funds to enjoy herself a little, it never dawned on Claudia to live it up a bit. She was too busy saving every red cent, making sure to secure her future and her mother's retirement.

Pulling away from the bed, Claudia rummage through her clothes. She had some pretty hot items; one's that would flaunt her shapely figure, but none that she could just go shopping in. She needed hip hugging destroyed denim jeans and a belly revealing top. As an alternative, Claudia settled on a thigh high one-piece dress and three-inch heels. Sliding into the bathroom, she hummed a little tune while she took a quick shower. The heat and force of the showerhead held her mesmerized for longer than it should have. Turning it off and stepping out, Claudia wiped the bathroom mirror and commenced to applying light foundation on her face.

Though it had been a long day, with work and dear ole Betsy breaking down on her, the four-hour power nap Claudia had on the flight over had given her an extra ounce of energy. She was feeling optimistic about her time with Jaden. Her phone tuned and she recognized the ring as his familiar set tone. Claudia glided to her cell.

"Hey you."

"Mi Amor, are you ready for me?"

The timbre of his voice sent a thrill of pleasure racing down her spine. *Was she ready for him?* Claudia's mind popped with the many ways she could be ready for him. All she needed was five seconds to drop this towel.

Jaden cleared his throat and reversed the question. "What I meant was, are you ready, chérie?"

Claudia imagined him licking those moist lips she'd wanted to stick her tongue between since the night he'd kissed her on their date. Tingles fled down her skin, and she shuddered. Suddenly, her voice was soft and sultry. "I'll be ready in five minutes."

"Take ten," his husky vocals rapped.

All I need is two seconds to drop this towel. Pressing her legs thinly together, Claudia was sure if this man didn't make love to her before the night was over, she'd be in the bathroom with the shower head between her thighs. *Lord have mercy.*

After fifteen minutes, Claudia twirled and twisted in the full-length mirror getting a three sixty view of her scantily clad dress. She was outfitted for a night on the town, not for shopping. Maybe they could do that tomorrow. She grabbed her clutch and sauntered to the door. Since Jaden had called her when she wasn't ready, this time she would be standing on his doorstep waiting for him.

But the action quickly dissipated when Claudia opened the door and found Jaden lying in wait; devastatingly handsome, in an all-black polo shirt that held two buttons, with the first one unhinged and a neatly folded collar. The casual short sleeves paused mid bicep and caressed his broad chest all the way down to his sculpted hips. The black trousers kissed his muscled thighs that rode down to a halt right above his ankles into a pair of loafers. A Rolex adorned his wrist, and sterling silver studs sat in each ear.

Claudia bit down on her lip. The confidence in his posture and the devilish gleam in his eye made her nipples pucker against the thin fabric she wore, setting off a flash of heat that journeyed to her panties. Jaden's gaze swept the length of Claudia, giving attention to her expresso brown silk legs and peek of her thigh that sprouted just an inch below the sequin dress she wore. When his perusal made it to her puckered breasts, they lingered there and his irises darkened with frank appreciation.

"Shit," he swore, reaching to gather her against his massive chest. Now with their lips separated by mere inches, Jaden spoke through a thick growl. "What are you trying to do to me in this dress?"

Claudia's mouth opened then closed, her thoughts shaken by the desire in his eyes. "I didn't bring anything casual to wear." Her voice was daunting and seductive.

Jaden's gaze faltered to her cherry lips, and Claudia could see an inner struggle swirling through his eyes like an earth-shattering hurricane. Claudia's breathing quickened, and the need to be with him in an erotically splay of passion overrode her ability to stay calm. Unabashed, she stuck her tongue out and licked his lips. That seemed to slip his resolve, and his mouth crashed into hers in a kiss that left her melting and panting for more. Claudia's hands slipped down to his trousers making haste to unbuckle his pants. Jaden reached down to cup her butt, lifting her in one effortless motion.

He pushed past her door to the king size surface of the bed where he laid her down gently, with his mouth tasting her hungry lips as if she would be dinner tonight. His mouth trailed down her chin to her neck where he sucked her warm skin.

Claudia moaned, "I need you now, Jaden."

Slowly he pulled back to gaze into her beautiful eyes.

"You said, if I needed you, you were just a knock away. Well, I need you, Jaden, right now, right here." Now that she'd made it clear what she desired, Claudia waited eagerly for him to respond.

"You are so beautiful," he said. Jaden's eyes roamed over the details in her features.

Claudia reached down and pulled her dress over her head, revealing a sexy lingerie set that exposed her chocolate nipples and freshly waxed mound. Jaden's fierce glare torched her nerves as he stared at her crotchless panties with lethal savagery. Like an animal savoring the meal before him, Jaden inched down, the strength in his corded muscles straining against his polo shirt. He lifted her legs and pulled her thighs against his broad shoulders spreading them wide.

A growl simmered from his lips as he took her pussy full on in his mouth. Immediately, Claudia arched her back and dug her nails into the spread of the sheets. Jaden's expert tongue lapped at her labia, going to and fro, relishing every drop of her.

"Sssssss, mmmm," Claudia moaned.

Jaden sucked on her clitoris threading a profound tongue and circling the sensitive flesh causing her toes to curl.

"Oh my God," she whimpered. Claudia's heart was raging against her breastbone, and she held on for dear life as an orgasm set on course.

She cried out again, "Jaden!"

He knew what her sharp cry indicated; she was on the verge of a climax. Reaching down, Claudia held the sides of his face bringing her body to a ninety-degree angle. Jaden's strong hands grazed up her thighs to the small of her back, and he kept his face between her thighs as he lifted her from the bed and hoisted her on his shoulders. With nowhere to run, Claudia moaned and purred, shouting and bucking. With ease, Jaden switched positions, glided to his back with Claudia now riding his face. His tongue held a never-ending whip on the folds of her erotic lips, and he smacked her ass.

A vibration of record breaking tremors assaulted her thighs, and Claudia's head fell back as an ear popping orgasm split through her core.

"Oh my God!" she yelled as quakes tore through her entire soul. Jaden was in heaven; sucking and slurping her sweet essence until there was not a drop left. With smooth ease, he gripped her hips and flipped her once again onto her back where she slumped into the heavy covers. With her breathing ragged and frazzled, Claudia reached desperately for him.

Jaden kissed up her thighs to her navel, sending a hot wave of nerves on a crash course. At her breasts, he sucked in a swollen nipple, licking and swirling his tongue in circles. Cupping her other breast, Jaden squeezed them together to take both of her chocolate areolas in his wet mouth.

Claudia pulled and tugged at his shirt wanting to relieve him of it. She needed him inside her yesterday. The numbing sensation between her thighs yearned for him, and he was taking his precious time. Jaden didn't want to disconnect from the warmth of her skin. He rejoiced in the fragrance of her flesh and the softness of her curves. He could lay between Claudia and sleep forever. He was drunk with lust, and the bulge in his pants was desperate to be inside her. But Jaden wasn't the happiest with himself at the moment.

His resolve had weakened too quickly. Claudia was doing something to him that had never been done before. When he was on a mission, rarely did he ever break. But Claudia had evidently capsized his ship, and he'd sunk into the depths of her watery seas and drowned in her ocean. His body was on fire and he'd barely been able to control the beast that stirred his soul.

When Jaden made love to Claudia in Puerto Rico, holding back his savagery was difficult then, but now there was barely any willpower left, and the prerequisite to be with her spiraled off him in an upsurge of craving. Without saying a word, Jaden pulled to rest on the haunches of his legs. Quickly his shirt flew over his powerful arms across the room. With his pants half unbuckled from Claudia's earlier ravishing, Jaden pulled the belt from his pants loops. It also went sailing across the suite.

Getting an eyeful of his powerfully male physique, Claudia bit down on her lip, her eyes dropping halfway. Jaden scooped her up in his arms and rolled her, pulling her back to his chest as they stretched out on the bed. As he spooned her, Claudia wondered if this was an intermission phase or if he was calling it quits and she was a bit perturbed.

Looking back into the pillar of his neck she spoke, "Is everything okay?" Claudia almost didn't recognize the thick vocals in her voice.

"Better than ever, chérie," his deep voice threaded.

Claudia turned to face him. "You should take these off then," she tugged at his pants. "I want to return the favor..."

A groan fled his lips at her naughty retort, but Claudia mistook it for something else.

"Are you sure everything's okay?"

His gaze found hers. "I wouldn't lie to you, chérie. Nothing could be better than this moment we've found ourselves in."

Jaden's words and actions didn't link up, and Claudia was severely confused.

"If you don't mind, I'd just like to hold you for a minute," his lips met hers, and he nibbled around her mouth, tracing the curves of her lips with his tongue. Claudia shivered and smiled, kissing him back. His response had calmed her spirits, and she'd gotten comfortable. Not too long after, Claudia was yet again sleeping like a baby. But Jaden was awake with thoughts of happily ever after assailing his mind. With his fingers, he walked them down her face and basked in the comfort of their cocoon.

Could he do it, be committed with her, forever? The notion didn't terrify him like it usually did. It confirmed what he'd been feeling and thinking over the last several days. Jaden wanted Claudia to bear his surname. To have an extended stay in her life seemed paramount. No other woman would do, now that he'd known her. And even though this was something that sat heavy on his heart, Jaden didn't want to scare her away. Nor did he want to give the impression that their relationship didn't go past the physical.

A plan began to formulate, and a grin spread across his lips. If it were up to Jaden, he would take his time. But the force that tied them together was stronger than he'd given credit. No matter what them being together entailed, Jaden would never let her go.

Chapter Sixteen

When Claudia's eyes drifted open, she was underneath a thick layer of cover. She rolled to find the other side of her bed vacant. A closer look revealed a note neatly folded with a chocolate rose on the pillow top. *Sweet treats early in the morning. I could get used to that.* Claudia reached for the note flipping it open.

Good morning, chérie. We have a full day ahead of us, so get dressed. Your clothes are laying across the chair next to the door. DON'T step out in a sexy ass dress like the one you had on last night or we will never see the Las Vegas sights.

Claudia couldn't help but roll her face into the sheets and laugh. It was true, they never made it shopping last night, and there were plenty of sexy dresses where that last one came from. She peered over to the clothes on the chair. A pair of jeans was the first thing she saw. Another wave of giggles bubbled from her and Claudia tossed the covers over her head and sighed. It didn't get past her that they never made it to round two, but she would solve that little problem soon enough. Her cell phone chimed with an incoming text message. Claudia's arm shot out of the cover and felt around for the device.

Pulling it underneath the sheets, Claudia opened the message from Samiyah.

Having a good time, I suppose, since I never received a call from you.

Claudia typed back.

Seeing as how I was ambushed you shouldn't be looking for a call from me.

The response came fast.

Oh please, don't act like you wouldn't rather be with him instead of me.

Claudia giggled.

True. But you still wrong for setting me up. I wasn't prepared to see his sexy ass. I was looking regular girl.

Another bing.

Ha! I'm sure you were fine. You can thank me later.

Claudia twisted her lips.

I probably will. Lol.

Claudia sent a smiling emoji behind her last text and tossed her phone to the side. Peeling back the covers, she slipped out of bed and strolled to the bathroom. "Okay," she said to herself, "Let's try this again."

Jaden and Claudia didn't have to venture out to go shopping. The Palazzo Hotel held the Grand Canal Shoppes; a destination on the Las Vegas Strip. The

Venetian inspired shopping center provided 160 trademark stores and prime luxurious brands with more than a dozen five-star restaurants. As they strolled down the brick lamented pathway, Claudia wondered how she'd missed this part of Las Vegas on her girls trip. But then, they couldn't afford to stay at a hotel like this, and she wouldn't dare take a trip into the high-end emporiums.

"This canal is beautiful," she said.

"Would you like to take a ride?" Jaden pointed to the gondola. "We can window shop and relax if you'd like."

"That would be blissful, but I probably should grab some clothes, since I only packed enough for a day." She turned to him stopping their forward progress. "You didn't say how long we'll be here, what did you have in mind?"

Jaden traced the outline of her face with his fingertip. "How long would you like to stay, chérie?" His voice was mellow and inviting.

"I supposed we couldn't stay forever?" Claudia gave a sheepish grin.

Jaden laughed out loud. "Unless you're willing to relocate your family and sell your part of S & M Financial Advisory, then I don't think we can."

Claudia pushed her lips out turning them up.

"What?" he said.

"I'm thinking about how long it would take to move."

Jaden laughed. "I could have your things packed and ready within three days."

Claudia's brows shot up in surprise. "Three days, huh?"

"Three days," he repeated.

"How would you pull off such a feat?"

"I have the means to do whatever you want."

"But it wouldn't be the same without you here," Claudia groaned.

"Who said I would be going anywhere?"

Claudia stared at him for a minute, a smile lifting her lips. She burst into laughter.

"Why do you find that funny?" He said; amusement in his eyes.

"I appreciate you living that dream with me for a moment. It was really nice of you."

"Dreams can become a reality, when you wish."

Claudia blushed, sliding her hand into the palm of his. Their fingers joined and Jaden held a light squeeze on them. *I need to snap out of it,* Claudia thought. But she didn't want to. Jaden wasn't making the plunge she was surely taking any easier. In fact, he made falling in love with him unpretentious. *Just get through this trip Claudia, and you can gradually separate yourself from him.*

"We should probably go inside."

Claudia tugged his arm pulling him along, ignoring the penetrating gaze he held on her. They strolled into Barney's and browsed around.

"Oh, this is nice."

Claudia held up a one-piece jumpsuit. The material felt like silk against her skin. She twisted her lips as she judged the piece of clothing.

"Maybe too tight on my hips though."

Jaden grabbed the jumpsuit out of her hands, "Only one way to find out." He scanned the retailer looking for signs of a changing room.

"I don't know..." Claudia whined.

"I've got a feeling I know exactly how it's going to fit."

"Do you?"

Jaden wiggled his eyebrows suggestively. "I do."

Claudia giggled. "Maybe we should wait until I have more items or this could be an all day, trip. Have you ever shopped with a woman before?"

"From what I was told when I was about nine years old with my mother."

Claudia twisted her lips. "That hardly counts."

"No?"

She shook her head. "No baby, I don't think it does."

Jaden didn't miss the endearment that left her mouth. It settled warmly inside him, and unable to resist, he reached out and touched her lips. The warm pad of his thumb caused Claudia to shudder, and the need to suck it in her mouth became immense. But as soon as the thought entered, Jaden dropped his hand and took a step back. His nostril flared, and he took his vision everywhere but her. Claudia peered at him, confused, then looked away. She moved along the aisles pretending to be absorbed in the catalog. But her mind was on him and what she would do about the flames that arose when being around him. After an hour of browsing and picking out clothes, Claudia made her way to the dressing room.

At the entrance, Jaden paused, and she turned to him. "Are you coming?"

"Inside the dressing room with you?"

"Yeah, I may need help with a zipper or two."

Jaden's eyes darkened, and his jaw tightened. In a husky voice, he spoke, "I don't think that's such a good idea, chérie."

Claudia loved it when he called her that, and she wondered if he called every woman he held up with the same.

"Why not?"

The unadulterated lust she saw in his eyes made her quiver and bite down on her lips.

"If you need help with," he paused, "with a zipper, step out and I'll assist."

Claudia pursed her lips. "Have it your way," she pivoted on her heels and sauntered into the dressing room.

Outside, Jaden patted himself on the back for declining her invitation. It wasn't easy and keeping himself in check was becoming impossible with every waking moment. Shit. He pulled his hand down his face. Why did Claudia get under his skin so bad? The chemistry was something he'd never felt before. When she exited the dressing room in the one-piece jumpsuit, it became apparent that keeping his hands to himself wasn't plausible.

"I told you this would be too tight on my hips."

Jaden's gaze roamed from her luscious lips down the length of her neck to the silk material that held up her breasts. They sat high as the jumpsuit squeezed them together and her hard nipples protruded through; beckoning him to suck them. The torch she'd certainly lit didn't diminish as his examination fell to her flat belly and audacious round hips.

"Take it off," his rough voice barked.

"Excuse me?"

Jaden cleared his throat. "I said," his eyes moved back to hers, "take... it... off."

Claudia squirmed under his fiery gaze. She swallowed as a tingle led a dance down her spine.

Dangerously, Claudia turned slowly, now exposing her derriere, "But you haven't had a chance to see the back yet."

Her voice was half vixen half purr. If Jaden didn't feel like a savage before, he felt it now. She was toying with him. Inside this store, prancing her little sexy ass in that suit.

"Do you really want to do that, Claudia?"

Claudia was feeling herself, and she was tired of him running from her. While she had the bravado, Claudia placed her arm against the wall and arched her back like a centerfold. She turned to look at him giving him the sexiest pose he'd ever seen in his life.

His feet moved, and Jaden was on her assembling Claudia into his arms with the viciousness of a lion needing to get to his lioness. He slammed his lips to hers, and they stumbled back into the dressing room. With his leg, Jaden closed the door. Once inside, he pulled Claudia by her ass off her feet to his pelvis. Her legs wrapped around his waist as her arms coiled around his neck and his fingers dug into the curve of her behind.

"Mmmm," she moaned as he kissed, sucked and pulled at her lips hungrily. Her breathing became bated, her chest rising and falling rapidly. Jaden pulled away from her lips to kiss down her jaw and neck. Every spot his warm wet mouth touched stirred a flame that burned through her flesh.

"Oh my God," she breathed, delighted in the absolute animal he'd become. Jaden sank the sharp edges of his teeth into her skin. The grip he held on her ass was tight and possessive. He'd tear her apart if given the chance and somehow Claudia knew in Puerto Rico, Jaden had held out on her. Their lovemaking that night had been soft and slow, but this Jaden was downright ravenous, and she wanted everything he had to offer.

It didn't help that the bulge pressing firmly into her crotch had soaked her panties and every second he held her she fell for him even harder. Someone entered the dressing room pulling them out of their erotic haze. Jaden didn't pull away instantly. His lips softly danced across her skin over the spots he'd bitten just moments before. Claudia closed her eyes and exhaled. Her libido was on fire, and she needed him so bad it was making her ill. When Jaden pulled away from her neck; their eyes met.

"What are you doing to me girl?"

His dark voice vibrated through her core. They were so hyper aware of each other that they could feel every breath and tremor bouncing between them. Jaden could feel the quick beat of her heart and she, his. The air around them held thick and warm.

"Whatever it is your doing to me," Claudia responded.

More people entered the dressing room, and children could be heard. Jaden set Claudia back down to her feet.

"Don't try on anything else. Let's get out of here before they put us out," he said.

"But nobody knows we're in here."

"You think it'll stay that way if we spend another minute behind these walls?"

Claudia swallowed visibly. "I suppose not."

Jaden reached for the stack of clothes behind her and slid his large hand in hers, leading Claudia away from the dressing room. At the register, Jaden gave the cashier his American Express Black Card.

"Um, I was going to pay for that," Claudia objected.

Jaden regarded her. "No you weren't."

She placed her hands on her hips. "Yes, I was."

Her feistiness just further turned him on. "Next time," he winked, although he had no intention of letting her pay for anything.

Leaving Barney's, they returned to Claudia's suite briefly so she could leave the bags inside. Jaden made sure to stand outside while she went in which confused Claudia further, but her unspoken questions were never raised.

They left the Palazzo hotel, and Claudia was silent the entire ride.

"Everything alright?" Jaden asked.

Claudia gave him a small smile. "Sure."

Jaden wasn't convinced. "You can talk to me, about anything."

Claudia shifted in her seat. "I could go on and on about whatever, so I'm sure you don't mean that."

"Then you're mistaken."

They held each other with their gazes. The mixed signals were becoming frustrating for her. Claudia decided to mess with him.

"Last week I had a hang nail that about made me scream, my big toe hurt so bad I ran to the nail salon to have it fixed. You should've seen it!"

Jaden threw his head back and roared a contagious laugh that made Claudia laugh in return. When his mirth whined down, a lazy grin replaced it. "I hardly doubt you had a hang nail."

"No?"

"Nice try but that was a good story."

Claudia stuck her tongue out and crossed her eyes, and another deep laugh escaped him. Witnessing her sense of humor was a breath of fresh air. Most of the women he'd dated were poised but haughty. They came from wealthy families, so the need to be self-made didn't interest them. It was endless. But Claudia was so refreshingly different he could see them together for all time. Thoughts of her loving and caring nature invaded his mind. With her being the youngest sister, Claudia had stepped up to take care of her mother when it was most needed, and ever since he'd known her, Jaden hadn't heard Claudia complain once.

Her business savvy was an extreme turn on for him and being a beautiful, seductress was an A plus. But what could he offer her? Money and luxury? Those things were great, but Jaden wanted to give her the whole shebang. The emotional support that came with loving and caring for a person. The mental and trustworthy stability that came with being in a monogamous relationship. The physical ability to make her body crave him in her sleep. Jaden was confident he could have that last part down, but what about everything else?

Was he ready, truly?

"Where are we headed?" Claudia asked interrupting his thoughts.

"To grab something to eat. Are you hungry?"

Not for food, Claudia thought but said, "A little."

Jaden reached over and touched her face. "Then we'll get something to fill your little appetite."

He had no idea that her appetite was anything but little. However, it involved him and the king size mattress back at her hotel room, but since he seemed to be playing hard to get, she'd leave him be, for now.

Chapter Seventeen

There was a light breeze in the Las Vegas atmosphere, and Jaden and Claudia managed to spend most of the day at a barbeque joint. Laughter and conversation had held them steady for what seemed like minutes but in actuality had been hours. Claudia had grown friendly with the manager immediately. It appeared that no man could resist her charm. She'd whispered something in the owner's ear, and he'd perked up.

"I would be delighted," he'd told her.

Puzzled, Jaden watched Claudia rise from her seat. "I'll be right back, handsome." She placed a tender kiss on his jaw and scurried off to the kitchen. When Claudia returned, she was skirted in a red apron with a bowl in her hand.

Returning with her, the manager sat down a rack of ribs that sizzled; holding a juicy moistness that made his stomach growl.

"This is my mother's secret sauce," Claudia informed him. She placed a piece of rib on his plate and doused it with the sauce. "If you like it, I'll give you more."

The thick honey smell assaulted his senses, and he immediately took a bite. Claudia watched him as he inhaled the fall of the bone meat. He made eating look like sex. Or maybe she was just horny. Either way, Claudia could watch him eat forever. When a single drop of sauce hit his chin, she'd wanted to lick it off with her tongue, but she held back.

"This is delicious. Your mother must be proud."

Claudia sucked her lips in. "She doesn't know I've learned it."

Jaden stopped chewing then swallowed the remainder of the meat that sat on his tongue. "How does she not know, she taught you, right?"

"I watched her thoroughly, but my mom and sister don't take me seriously, so I just kept it to myself. I have a habit of doing that."

"Keeping things to yourself?"

"Yes."

"Why?"

"To guard myself I supposed."

Jaden considered her for a long moment. "And what things are you keeping from me?"

Claudia wasn't prepared for that question even though she'd stepped right into it. A plethora of thoughts ran through her mind, but she said none of them.

Stumbling she said. "No- nothing."

There was unease in her response, and Jaden knew she was keeping something from him, but he reverted to her initial reply to give her a break. *Later*, he thought, *we'll get to it later.*

"Why don't you talk to them about it? I think your mom will listen."

Claudia twisted her lips. "And Desiree?"

"One at a time. We'll work on her."

Claudia laughed, and they sat and ate.

"There is something I've wanted to ask you about," Claudia confessed.

Jaden sat his rib down and looked on eagerly.

"You have my attention," he said.

"I've lived in Chicago all of my life and as famous as your family is, I didn't hear a lot about you growing up. It was only when I was in my twenties that I began to see you on TV or in the newspapers. I mean, I know we run in different circles with me growing up in the hood and all but I just—"

Claudia rambled, and Jaden's hands touched her arm. The heat from his palm made her shiver. She stopped speaking instantly at his touch.

"Ask your question, chérie," he said.

Claudia swallowed her tongue.

"Umm, well I guess I want to know where you were in your earlier years. What was life like for you?"

Jaden sat back in his seat and mused over her question. He grabbed a glass of water and took a large sip.

"I can only account for the last twenty years of my life," he sighed.

Claudia's eyes widened.

"I was ten years old when my mother passed away. It was a home invasion. At the time, the only people in the house were me, Josiah, my mother, and my sisters who were upstairs in their crib. Jonas had gone to the store and Julian, Jonathon, and Jordon, were outside playing around. When the men came in, they wore ski masks, and held big guns. You would think we had drugs in our home with the way they rushed the house."

Jaden took another sip of water.

"I saw them from the banister on the second floor. When they kicked in our front door, it was earsplitting, like a crack of lightning. I ran to my father's cabinet, where he kept his rifles and pulled one off the shelf. Josiah was too young to carry one, so it was up to me to protect us."

Jaden paused, his eyes dropping to the food that sat in front of him as he stared off into space.

"I ran up on the tallest one with my gun aimed at his head. I could've taken the shot, but I failed to check the rest of the house first. One of his partners hit me over the head with the butt of his gun, and I passed out. When I came to, Jonas was standing over me, and Josiah was standing next to him."

Jaden's voice imitated the younger version of himself. "Did you get em?" I asked Jonas.

"No, get up you have to help me find, Jonathon, Julian, and Jordan." He said. "He was panicked, and at the time, I didn't know our mother wasn't alive."

Claudia covered her mouth with her hand.

"To make an extremely long story short. I haven't been able to remember anything since that day. Memories of my mother before that point are a blur. I thought I was being punished for not living up to the hero I know I could've been. And although I know Jonas feels responsible because he's the oldest, I'm the next in line, and I was there. I've had to live with the guilt of not saving my mother, and for a long while, I wouldn't speak. As my family's reputation grew, I made sure to stay out of the limelight. With my father and brother's help of course. We all carry a bit of the traumatic event but none more than me."

"Jaden..." Claudia said. "You sound as if you still blame yourself. You were ten years old. It's not your fault."

Jaden offered Claudia an easy smile. "I know that now."

"But you still feel responsible."

"Of course, I'm a man, sure I was a boy then, but that's no excuse. I can take it in stride now. I don't dwell on it or have pity parties. But to answer your question, that's the reason you didn't see much of me. It was only when Jonas took me under his wing did I show an interest in anything outside of my head. It took me five years before I spoke my first word again. Jonas and I were playing basketball in the garage as my other brothers looked on from the sideline. I'd made the three-point shot winning the game. I screamed. Yeaaah! And my brother's all turned to me, surprised." Jaden chuckled. "I was kind of surprised, too. That was a beautiful day. I wasn't completely myself again, but I would say something here and there. Another five years passed and I was Jaden again, except for the fact that the only memory I have of my mother is her death."

Jaden went quiet again and this time Claudia spoke up.

"Are you the one who started her foundation?"

"I proposed the idea but we all contributed to making it a reality. Jan's Roses, named after my mother, Janet. Devoted to assisting victims' families of home invasions. My brother, Jonathon runs it."

"I admire you," Claudia said. "You are a fearless man, Jaden. You were then, and you are now. Some people don't come back when they go through tragedy. You are loved unconditionally, and your support system is strong. I'm sure your mother is happier than anything that you survived. And you're going to be an excellent father and make some woman lucky one day." She smiled, "I'll place a bet on that."

I guess you'll find out Jaden thought. The turn of his thoughts pulled at Jaden's chest. He tried to dismiss the sudden promise. But it refused to go away. He smiled at her, and their conversation remained light for the remainder of the evening. There was still a twinge of spicy barbeque on their lips when they decided to take their leave.

Now standing on a field of green grass, nervous energy surrounded Claudia as she stared at the largest balloon she'd ever seen. In awe at the size of it, she turned to Jaden. "Have you ever ridden a balloon ride before?"

"I can't say that I have." He slid his arm around her shoulders. "Are you worried?"

Instead of pretending, she admitted outright, "Yes, I am."

Watching her intensely had become second nature for Jaden, he loved that she was so fascinated like a kid on Christmas. The guide approached with his hand held out. "Good evening, you must be Mr. Rose."

"Yes sir," Jaden shook his hand, "And this is—"

"Mrs. Rose," the guide spoke up without giving Jaden a chance to finish.

When Jaden didn't correct the guide, Claudia turned to him flustered.

"Mrs. Rose," Jaden said a gleam in his eyes, "This way."

Claudia blushed but also made no mention of correction; she could pretend to be the misses for however long he wanted. They strolled to the hot air balloon and Jaden helped her inside. The guide didn't do much talking as the heat shot out of the mechanical device causing the balloon to take flight, but he did make some small comments.

"You're just in time for this miraculous sunset," the guide said. "In about five minutes you'll get the best view of Las Vegas yet."

Claudia leaned into Jaden, snuggling under his warmth. His male scent did erotic dances across her nose, and she exhaled. Being with him was exhilarating, and Claudia never wanted this time with him to end. Rubbing an affectionate hand over her back, Jaden bent his head and kissed her temples then slowly turned her to face the view. Claudia gasped.

"Wow, this is extraordinary."

"It is," Jaden responded. He held her tighter against his wide chest, and Claudia's head fell against him. A swirl of wind flew around them and this moment was heaven for them both.

Claudia hadn't been with a man like Jaden; respectful, charismatic, thoughtful, wealthy, caring. Hell, she hadn't been with a man long enough to grow anything real. Her relationships had been more like scattered thunderstorms. The mountains surrounding the Las Vegas Strip were large and rose by every moment of their ascent.

"Here it comes," the guide said.

The skyline ignited as an array of orange stretched across the clouds. Claudia gasped again pulling slightly away from Jaden.

"My God," she whispered softly. If only she could take this moment and bottle it up to re-live later. The sunset cast a glow over the Las Vegas scenery, and Claudia turned to look at Jaden only to find him gazing intently at her.

"Are you seeing this, you're going to miss this view."

"On the contrary, chérie, I have the best view in my sights already."

His arm slid back around her waist, drawing her into him. A kiss that sparked like a soft flame, smooth and warm, became predatory and detrimental within seconds. Claudia became unhinged. In her sights all she saw was him. His honey brown eyes and sculpted features in front of an orange display of the heavens. Claudia skimmed her hands up his chest and pulled slightly away.

"You have to stop doing this."

Jaden cleared his throat. "What if I can't?"

They stared at each other. Claudia was trying to decipher what he was getting at and Jaden awaited her response. Finally, Claudia turned away from him placing her hands on the basket's edge. With the sun finally setting, their balloon flight began to descend. What did he want from her? Why was he so primitive one second and pulling away from her the next? One thing was for sure, Claudia had played enough games with men to last a lifetime, and she could no longer deny that she'd fallen in love with Jaden.

She inhaled a deep breath and pushed it out just as hard. Trying to get him out of her system once they'd made it back to Chicago was going to be dreadful. When their ride cruised back to the ground, Claudia was the first out. She could hear Jaden saying something to the guide before he sprung into a jog to catch up to her.

"Hey," he grabbed her arm turning her to face him. "Did I do something wrong?"

The concern on his face didn't make her unstable emotions calm. "I'm fine," she said.

But he knew better. "You're keeping something from me, Claudia. Tell me what it is."

"I told you I'm fine, okay? Can we just go back to the hotel? I need some water."

He watched her walk away then went after her again. At the car, they climbed in and Jaden turned the engine. Claudia was avoiding his gaze. She bit down on the inside of her jaw and twiddled her thumbs that sat in her lap.

"Seat belt," he said.

Unsteady, Claudia fumbled with the seatbelt, but it was stuck. The tug and pull on the leather strap did her no good since it wouldn't budge. Jaden reached over placing a warm hand over hers to steady her motions.

"Let me help you," his deep voice thrummed through her. The rise and fall of her chest practically rocked her as his closeness played a game with her nerves. Jaden needed to know what had set her off. Pulling the strap, it stretched with ease as he buckled it around her. But Jaden didn't move back. He hovered at her side watching her.

"Do you want to talk about it?"

"What is there to talk about?" Claudia kept her eyes straight out the window as she spoke.

"Chérie..."

"Don't," she said.

He continued to read her. "Will you at least tell me what I did wrong, so that I won't do it again?"

Claudia's pulse kicked up a notch.

"I just need to get some water and settle down." Finally she gave him eye contact. "It's me, not you."

Bewildered, Jaden sat back in his seat, "Really?"

Claudia understood how she sounded. "I mean, it must have been the ride and all my crazy thoughts. I just need to get some water."

Jaden knew Claudia was holding back from him. Relaxing a bit, he put the car in reverse and pulled off the gravel to the road.

They rode in silence back to the Palazzo hotel. Standing in front of her suite Jaden spoke.

"Claudia whatever it is that you're feeling, don't hold it back from me. We're getting to know one another, right? No holding back."

That was easy for him to say, she thought. He wasn't the one falling in love when they were friends with benefits. But since they'd left Puerto Rico, the benefits portion of this friendship had become obsolete, since every time Claudia thought they would have sex, Jaden withdrew. She didn't know what to think, but she did know she wanted and needed to connect with him.

"Would you like to come in?"

"If you'll have me."

She turned to insert her key card. The pad on the door struck green, and they walked inside. Housekeeping had obviously made their rounds since the bed Claudia left ruffled was now just as sharp as it was when they checked in.

Going straight to the bar, Claudia pulled a short glass from the counter and added two cubes of ice.

"Would you like something to drink?" Claudia asked.

"What do you have?"

"Well let's see."

Claudia bent to eye the display of liquors calling them out one at a time and giving Jaden a full view of her round, voluptuous backside.

"Let me help you with that," he said appearing behind her like he'd been conjured.

Claudia stood slowly, indulging in the warmth of his body heat. Her pulse spiked, and she chugged the glass of water. It did nothing to calm her raging libido. Jaden reached for a glass and poured brown liquor on top of two cubes.

"Feeling refreshed?" He asked glancing to her empty glass of water.

"Hardly," she chuckled.

"More?"

"I don't think the water is going to suffice."

"You have wine, or perhaps..." he offered her the liquor pointing the bottle at her glass.

It was probably the last thing she needed, but she went for it anyway.

"Just a shot."

That one shot turned into two.

"Can you handle it?" Jaden asked.

"Can you?"

Jaden's brows rose. Somehow, he knew they were no longer speaking in terms of the liquor.

"I beg your pardon?"

"Can you handle it?" Claudia took a step forward.

His voice dipped an octave. "I can handle all things, chérie."

"Oh yeah?"

"Yeah..."

"Prove it."

Claudia removed the blouse she wore. It sailed off her fingertips with ease. Her hands glided down her bare belly unsnapping the clasp on the jeans she wore. Moving her hips side to side in a strip tease, Claudia peeled the denim jeans down her thighs and legs. Stepping out of them, she kicked them to the side. Jaden's gaze darkened and his jaw tightened.

"I want," Claudia slipped her hands behind her back and unclasped her bra, "you." She pulled the straps off her shoulders and tightened her arms around her breasts that were still covered by the lacy material, "In the worst way." She bent her head and licked the lace covering that sat on top of her dark brown areolas. "Can you handle it, Jaden?"

If there was any resolve left in Jaden, it had officially shattered. He slammed the glass down on the counter and took one step before snatching her in his arms. He carried her to the bed and laid her down. His lips met her smooth skin leading a trail down her shoulders. Claudia tugged at his shirt wanting desperately to feel his ripped abs against hers. He pulled the material over his head, and she flung it across the room.

"Shit, girl," he hovered over her adoring every inch of her flesh. "You shouldn't have done that." He cursed. "So fucking beautiful."

Claudia's pulse was racing. "Why not?" she asked. "What's been stopping you? You've been standoffish what's up with that? If you don't want me, just say that and stop playing with my emotions."

Jaden crushed his mouth to hers, and a stabbing heat bounced between them landing between their centers. Jaden stretched her mouth with his tongue; invading the warm wetness of her palette. They moaned, and he removed the lace material that still separated him from her chocolate breasts. Dragging his lips down her jaw, Jaden nibbled on her neck before dropping his lips to her nipples. Massaging one while inhaling the other, his expert tongue lapped like she was the last chocolate snack on earth.

Claudia stretched and moaned, rising off the bed just enough to meet his pelvis. Her fingers drifted up the back of his head.

"Now, Jaden and don't hold back."

Jaden sucked in the other breast showing them both equal devotion.

Claudia moaned again, "Now... now..."

His massive hands skated down her hips to find the string of her panties. With fervor, Jaden pulled, and the lace snapped causing her body to bounce. Claudia's heartbeat built momentum as his mouth found her sex. His tongue hadn't been on her ten seconds before her legs began to quiver.

"Now... now... now..." she continued to pant. But Jaden was taking his precious time, savoring the taste of her cream like it was surely his last meal. A rumble left his throat, and it caused a vibration to crawl throughout her.

"My God," she panted. If he could send her into oblivion like this, Claudia could only imagine what he could do if he let go of his inhibitions. As hard as it was for Claudia to pull away, she scurried toward the headboard officially out of his grasp.

Like a wildlife creature, Jaden pulled his face up to look at her. His eyes glowed with an unruly illumination that Claudia had never seen before. It should've scared her to death, but it only awakened the animal that lie within her.

"Where are you going?" His dark voice rumbled.

Knowing she was teetering on a dangerous course of action but not caring, Claudia turned with the grace of a cat to her knees propping her dark chocolate ass in the air. As she settled on all fours, her legs parted an inch more, making sure he got the full look at her lips below.

"I said..." Claudia purred, "Now, Jaden."

There was movement on the bed, and a second later Claudia was being dragged from the headboard to the bed's edge. Claudia tossed a glance over her shoulder in time to see Jaden ripped a foiled package with his teeth. Seconds later, a profound intrusion stretched her wide plummeting to perilous depths.

Her mouth fell open as a wounded wail left her vocal cords. She attempted to move, and Jaden laid a rough hand around her waist.

"Nah," he said, his voice laced with venom. "You don't get to run." He buried himself inside her. Claudia's ass now at the base of his pelvis. She didn't move for fear her death would come quickly. She barely even breathed. Jaden reached forward bending slightly over her making his intrusion even more detrimental. His powerful hand tightened around her throat pulling her back on her knees. Claudia's breath was labored, and her pulse beat out of control. With her back now against his chest, Jaden placed his lips to her ear trailing the lobe with his tongue.

"Are you scared, chérie?"

Gathering her strength, Claudia drew in a shuddered breath. Instead of giving him a direct answer, she opted to play with her life.

"Why should I be, Jaden? It's not like you're going to murder meeeee!"

Stars were dancing around her vision as Jaden pulled out of her slippery folds only to drive back inside her with barely restrained barbarism. His grip tightened around her neck and with his other hand he smacked her bottom and Claudia tumbled forward.

She moaned, and her toes curled as he tunneled in and out of her; their momentum increasing by the second. Before long, Claudia's moans turned into shouts. Sounds of skin slapping against skin penetrated the room. The hold on her throat became dangerous, but the sensation coupled with Jaden's savagery felt so incredible Claudia didn't care if she passed out.

Recognizing his strength, Jaden loosened his grip just a bit, but it didn't stop the headboard from knocking against the wall.

"Is this what you wanted, Claudia?"

Claudia couldn't put together a word let alone a complete sentence. A whimper fell from her lips, and Jaden's temerarious speed increased.

"Aaaaaah! Jaden! Jaden!"

He released her neck, and his fingers dug into her waist. While Claudia tried to scurry, he held on firm lifting the bottom half of her in the air giving her every wicked inch she'd asked for.

"Do you want me to stop, chérie?"

More whimpering fell from Claudia's lips as she became more delirious by the second. When his question went without a response, Jaden crawled onto the bed while pumping into her shaken body. Claudia's knees never touched the bed as he hoisted them around his waist. Jaden's mouth kissed up her back as he dug into her vagina sending an orgasm shooting through Claudia's core. She screamed and mumbled something unintelligible as her head sunk into the bed. His teeth bore into her shoulder, and a rumble left his throat.

"See what you did?" he said. "I wanted to show you, Claudia. Show you that you mean more to me than just a summer fling. I tried to show you, that our connection goes beyond a sexual encounter. But you wouldn't hear it, would you?"

Jaden continued to rock into her sending spasms on a sprint that shook them both.

"Fuck!" he yelled. "You wanted the monster inside of me; you got it."

Rising to his knees, Jaden's notorious hands gripped Claudia's ass spreading her cheeks even further. Claudia shrieked and came again, convulsions racking her body violently. She was unable to warn him. She was unable to do anything but take the beat down she'd asked for.

Jaden dipped and dug his stringent erection; knocking down her walls demolition style. A choked sob, left Claudia and she shut her eyes tight as tears streamed down her face.

Mistaken her tears as a sign of pain, Jaden removed himself instantly and coupled her in his arms.

"Come here," he whispered, "I'm sorry, I didn't mean to hurt you." He kissed her closed lids then her cheeks. "Talk to me, baby." With a hand, Jaden massaged her inner thigh and Claudia trembled in his embrace.

Her tears didn't derive from pain but the beautiful ravishing of his love making united with the words he'd spoken.

"Why?" she asked.

Jaden was confused by her question. "Elaborate, chérie."

"You said what we have goes past a sexual encounter. Why would you want more than that with me?"

Baffled, Jaden continued to stroke her thighs. "Open your eyes."

But Claudia didn't want to look at him and see the disgrace that would surely show on his face. She turned away and buried her face in the down feathered pillow. "I don't deserve you, Jaden, not in any way except this one."

Stunned by her confession, Jaden quickly turned her to face him lifting her chin. "You've got to be kidding me, right?"

Claudia sighed, her insecurities and sour attitude had ruined the mood. "I'm sorry, just forget everything I said,"

Claudia attempted to straddle him, "Let me return the favor." She pulled to her knees.

Jaden placed a firm hand over hers. "You can't say something like that and ask me to forget about it. I need to know, what is this about?"

"Please, Jaden don't let me ruin the mood further, I just want to make you feel as good as you've made me feel."

Claudia struggled to mount him, but Jaden held firm. "Chérie..."

Claudia's movements stilled, and her eyes met his.

"Talk to me. What is this about?"

Claudia sighed and sank to the side of him. Her heart beat fast, and she covered her face with her hands. Gently, Jaden removed them, and again her eyes met his.

"I grew up on the opposite side of the tracks, Jaden. I was always in trouble, sometimes in and out of juvenile. With the solid reputation your family has, I just don't fit. I guess what I'm trying to say is, a man of your stature doesn't date women like me. Sex, sure, but a relationship?" Claudia twisted her lips.

Jaden pulled Claudia closer. "You need to know, first, that I am not superior to you." Claudia turned her face away, and Jaden turned it back. "Do you understand me? I don't ever want to hear you speak like you're beneath me just because your path in life was different than mine or anyone else's. You are beneath no one." His gaze bore into her. "Secondly, I don't give a damn what men of my stature, as you put it, tend to do. I am my own man, Claudia. Anyone would be lucky to claim you as their own. And it's a shame that I beat them to the punch because you're mine now."

Jaden dragged her on top of him; cloaking his mouth with hers. Claudia moaned into his lips as tingles spread up her spine. She'd heard everything he said, and now Claudia wanted more than ever to reconnect with him. More tears ran down her face, and Jaden kissed them all away. Effortlessly, Claudia slid on top of him easing down on his semi erect shaft as a mix of love and euphoria took over her. Jaden cursed as the warmth of her juices showered him and his fingers crawled up her neck into her curly tendrils. Claudia moved slowly at first, but her flow became bolder, and she braced her palms against his rugged chest.

Her mouth fell open as he grew harder, longer, and his girth widened inside her, "Oh my God, you feel so good," she panted.

Jaden pulled her down to meet his lips, and he devoured her mouth. His hands dug into her waist moving her hips faster, plunging in and out of her tight vagina.

Claudia's head fell back, and her nails dug into his flesh. Her moans turned into jumbled mumbles, and although she was on top, it was he that rocked her boat. In a smooth flip, Jaden was on top of her with Claudia's legs stretched against his biceps.

"Aaaah my God," she moaned. "You are so incredible…"

Jaden's lips kissed along her belly; his teeth, digging into her skin. Claudia had never had sex like this before.

Usually, teeth were a turn off for her. But Jaden only made her feel divine and every time his pearly white fangs gripped her, the wetter she became. A dizzy spell fell over her and Claudia knew this next orgasm would be her undoing.

Jaden's proficient tongue pulled against her bruised lips, and she opened her mouth to him in a scolding kiss.

"Mmmmm," Claudia moaned.

Jaden's mouth was abrasive and elaborate; combing back down her body with worship like it was his religious duty. Claudia's body vibrated, and Jaden roped his muscled arms around her possessively.

"Come with me, chérie."

A strangled scream left Claudia as they soared together; pants and moans, murmurs of gratitude and praise falling from their lips. The convulsions were plenty, leaving their bodies flanked with tingles. Jaden rolled to the side of her turning Claudia with him. They were still connected since neither of them wanted to part just yet.

"That was," Claudia panted, "Sensational. Where have you been all of my life?"

A husky laugh cajoled from his lips. "I could ask you the same, chérie."

Claudia snuggled closer although they were practically wall to wall. I love you. She gasped and covered her mouth, thinking she'd spoken the words out loud.

Jaden eyed her carefully, his brows furrowed. "What is it?"

Claudia sighed a huge relief after realizing she had indeed thought the words and not spoken them. "Oh nothing, I was mistaken."

"Are you sure?"

"Yes, trust me, everything is fine."

He kissed her forehead and Claudia thought about what a colossal mistake it would've been to say those forbidden words. Yes, Jaden said she was all his, but that didn't mean love.

Claudia had questions that needed answers but now was not the time to go into a conversation about them. So she shut her eyes to drown out her thoughts, hoping that tomorrow morning he would still be lying next to her.

Chapter Eighteen

The rise of the early morning sun pulled Jaden out of his slumber. Bare smooth shoulders rested against his lips and warmth curled within his abdomen from Claudia's heated skin. He was naked and so was she, lying cocooned in his arms. The covers were draped across their waist as the rest of them lay on full display. Soft snores rang out like saccharine tones and a plush bottom arched into Jaden's pelvis causing his manhood to leap. Jaden moved his lips slightly down Claudia's shoulders to the back of her neck. A soft moan escaped her before her snores returned.

Last night, their lovemaking had gone particularly unusual. For Jaden, sex had always been the means to a sweet release, and he'd reciprocated that to his lover. But what he'd experienced last night with Claudia was something more. He'd told her she was his and those words he meant, but he almost didn't know how to go about making that a fact.

It had never been in his interest to claim anyone. That woman would come before anything or anyone in his life; much like his father did his mother. Looking down at Claudia now, a solid tug pulled at his heartstrings. She was the humblest person he knew. It still shocked him that she felt unworthy. Of what, he was still trying to figure out. Jaden intended to show her otherwise every moment they were together.

The many late nights of telephone conversations had revealed that Claudia's relationships with men were rocky in the past. And she never spoke of her father. Jaden was determined to get down to the bottom of her lowly thoughts, and if Adeline or Desiree had anything to do with it, he would set them straight. Especially, if they would become future family. Jaden's head jerked back, that last thought dinging like an alarm inside his head. Family? He pondered on the idea for a moment when Claudia shifted and turned to face him with her eyes still closed.

Love, adoration, a sense of peace fell over him. *Damn*, he thought. He loved her. His mind whirled at the heaviness of what that meant. Not only did he love her, he wanted her, forever. But could he do it? Take the actual plunge into marriage? He almost wanted to shake off the heavy-laden thoughts. But then Claudia opened her eyes and a world of images of what could be, snapped through Jaden's mind before he could reject the idea. Her lips curved into a beautiful smile as the afterglow of love settled on her face.

"You're still here..."

"Where would you rather me be, chérie?"

Claudia loved the sound of his deep voice.

"The last time, you were gone."

Jaden offered her a lazy grin. "The last time, I was trying to keep my hands to myself."

Claudia's fingers playing with his chin. "And now?"

"Good luck with getting me to keep away from you."

Claudia giggled and kissed the side of his jaw.

"Would you like to shower with me, I can call up room service, and we'll have breakfast within the hour," he offered.

"I would love that."

Jaden's lips touched her forehead, the bridge of her nose, and finally her mouth. Warm tingles sparked when they touched, making it difficult for either of them to pull away.

"What would you like to do today?"

If left up to Claudia they would spend the entire next few days in this bed. She wanted to be totally spent by the time they went back to Chicago.

"Nothing would please me more than to spend more time in bed with you."

A debonair smile cruised across his lips. "Mmmm, I was thinking the same thing." Claudia giggled, stuffing her head in the nape of his neck.

Jaden's hands fiddled up and down her bare back, leaving trails of tingles, sparks, and flames to ravish her completely.

"You know if we shower, it may take us a minute to get out."

"Are you saying you would seduce me in the shower, Claudia?"

More giggles left her. "Hey, this is what happens when I'm happy and with a man that I adore."

Jaden pulled back to gaze at her. "You adore me, Claudia?"

Lord, she loved when he spoke her name like that. Claudia paused half emboldened and half afraid to tell him how she really felt.

"Yes."

Her voice was just below a whisper. "I'm sorry, I didn't catch that," he said.

Claudia let out a resigned sigh, "Yes, Jaden. I adore you." She watched him carefully trying to gauge his visual response. His gaze exposed nothing and then, another glorious smile curved up his sexy masculine lips.

"Does being with me make you happy, chérie?"

Claudia's heartbeat sped up, maybe she'd said too much. It wasn't ideal for her to share her emotions with anyone. Especially him. Her tongue slid across her lips before she spoke, "Yes." Her head fell from his gaze, and her insecurities were back on display.

He lifted her chin like he always did when Claudia looked away.

"There's no need to be nervous around me, but it's quite normal to feel cautious."

That was easy for him to say, she thought.

"What about you, Jaden. Are you happy when you're with me?"

Jaden squeezed her tighter. "The happiest I've been in a long while."

Claudia's heart raced.

"I've never wanted to be with someone so bad, Claudia. What do you think that means?"

Claudia knew what she wanted it to mean, but still, she wouldn't speak it.

"You tell me," she said wanting to put him on as much of a display as he'd done to her.

Jaden smirked. "Means I might never let you go." They eyed one another. "What do you think about that?"

Claudia put a defiant hand on her hips. "Might?" She huffed and rolled away from him jokingly, and he pulled her back into his arms. Claudia squealed as she continued her getaway but was locked firmly against his chest.

"You know what I mean woman; there's no getting away from me now."

His mouth kissed behind her lobe and danced down her neck, one graze after the other. Claudia's getaway paused, and she relaxed, mesmerized by the unadulterated lava that consumed her with his touch.

"If you keep this up we may not make it to the shower," Claudia purred.

"Oh, we'll make it," Jaden said. "Might not be now, but we will make it."

They settled back into each other with Jaden lifting her leg and entering her from the side.

"Aaaaah," Claudia moaned arching her back into him.

Jaden's teeth bared down on her neck sending a fire exploding through her nerves.

"Mmmm, that feels so good," she purred as he thrust in and out of her wet heat.

189

"Tell me how good, chérie."

Jaden's hand crept up her bare belly, his fingers circling a hardened nipple.

"Feels incredible, babe. I want you all the time."

"Then you'll have me," he promised, tightening his hold on her. Jaden's thrusts became more volatile as he stroked long and hard. Claudia felt deliciously saturated by his love. The throb between her legs making her tighten her vaginal walls around his hardness.

"Shit," he cursed as a ripple of heat covered him. His fingers slid into her hair, and he kissed down the back of her neck. Claudia shivered, opening her legs wider. Jaden bluntly pushed inside her, and a moan clawed from her throat. His even thrusts turned into a full-on plow.

"Oh my God, baby, baby, baby…"

"Yes love, tell me what you want."

"I'm sorry," she said, "I'm going to come."

A low, dark laugh left him, and his speed increased.

"Come for me, chérie."

Claudia's eyes rolled to the back of her head, and her heart thundered in her chest. Jaden removed himself and dropped down between her legs, lapping her creamy sweetness until there was none left. Claudia had lost her mind. Her body shook so violently; a heart attack was surely on the horizon.

After Jaden had licked her dry, Claudia lay spent, convulsions still racking her soul.

"Oh my God, I can't stop," she said.

Jaden rose back to her, enveloping Claudia tightly in his arms. His mouth touched her lips, then neck as Claudia's trembles slowed. She pulled her eyes to him in awe. A blissful haze washing over her.

"I can have sex with you for the rest of my life and never regret one second of it," she said, surprised her lips were moving. "Did I just speak English" she asked, and Jaden roared.

"No habla Española," he said, pretending she had indeed spoken another language.

Claudia gasped, and Jaden fell out laughing again. She swatted him when she remembered she didn't speak Spanish, either. That didn't mean his love didn't make her want to speak another language.

"I'm just messing with you, chérie." Jaden pulled himself to his knees and held a hand out to her. "Come, let's shower."

"I can't feel my legs."

Jaden pulled back a sexy grin. Leaning in, he massaged her legs and thighs with his callused hands.

"How about now?"

Claudia moaned. "Yessss, just like that." Her head rolled side to side. Claudia felt spineless under Jaden's touch. "This is not making me want to get up," she said.

"How about, we take a bubble bath instead?"

"Oh yes, that sounds nice."

"I thought you might like that."

Moving to his feet, Jaden disappeared into the bathroom but not before Claudia got an eyeful of his tush. She heard the water turn on, and she relaxed further in the sheets. This moment was so blissful it pained her to think of its end. But if her life continued like it always had, all good things came to an end.

The bubble bath had taken Claudia out. She and Jaden lounged in it for more than an hour with the suds soaking their bones in the calming, heated, claw foot tub. While she slept against Jaden's chest. He planned the day out in his head. Claudia would love Le Reve, a popular show in Las Vegas. He could see her eyes popping out right now, and it caused him to chuckle.

Easing out of the tub and gently laying Claudia's head against the back of it, Jaden strolled to the bedroom and called for room service then set a time for a car service to pick them up from the hotel. When Claudia awakened, Jaden sat to her side with a towel draped over his shoulder.

"How long was I asleep?"

"About an hour, give or take."

"Feels like half the day."

Jaden chuckled. "Almost."

Claudia gasped horrified. "Are you kidding?"

Jaden bent to kiss her lips. "We're on vacation. You can sleep as long as you want. Surely you need it."

"Yeah, but the last thing I want to do is sleep when I'm with you." Claudia tucked her head and covered her mouth. She was speaking her mind more every minute that passed.

Jaden smiled. "You talk as if you'll never spend time with me again, chérie."

Claudia decided not to respond. There was no telling what would come out of her mouth next. *I love you*, she thought. That definitely couldn't come out. How embarrassed would she be when he would most likely respond with something like thanks?

"Did you order room service?"

Jaden took note that she ignored his question. "Yes, if you're ready to get out of that tub, I'll feed you, after I dry you off."

Claudia lifted a brow. "You mean, figuratively right?"

Jaden shook his head slowly. "No, I don't."

This was another first for Claudia. If a boyfriend had asked her if he could dry her off before, she would've reared her head and shooed him away. But somehow, the thought of Jaden's forceful hands all over her skin indirectly or otherwise hardened her nipples and sent a thread of heat to her now throbbing sex. *Lord have mercy. This man is going to be the death of me*, she thought as she pulled herself to a stand.

Claudia watched him, as he watched the water spill from her shoulders and hips. His eyes trailed along her bare belly, and he licked his lips unknowingly. When his gaze landed on her smooth-shaven mound, Jaden moved, powerless to resist her pink clitoris that stuck out beckoning to be sucked. His mouth covered her pussy, and his tongue dug into her lips.

Claudia shrieked and buckled, but Jaden caught her before she could descend. She didn't think she could take another whipping from his talented tongue, but she did. Moaning on the verge of hysteria. Claudia called out to God and begged Jaden for mercy. He'd lifted her, hoisting her on his shoulders as he polished off what had become his regular nourishment.

"Oh. My. God. I'm coming!"

And boy did she come, hard and fast. Her brain short circuited, and she was speaking in tongues again. After washing her with a warm towelette, Jaden carried her into the room and laid her on the bed.

Inside, the room service trays were already present and covered. Claudia closed her eyes for a moment to gain her bearings.

"Do you need anything?"

Claudia opened an eye. "Trust me; you've given me everything I need at the moment."

Jaden chuckled. "Maybe you should put something on your stomach."

Claudia sat up seductively. "Mmmm, perhaps you're right."

She moved to sit in front of him pulling his boxer briefs over his toned hips. Jaden eyed her as she took the length of his arousal in her mouth.

His voice grew gruff. "That's not exactly what I had in mind but..."

His words were cut off at the suction of her lips.

"Shiiiiiiiiiit!"

His muscles clenched as Claudia worked up and down his shaft opening her throat to take in the most of him. Jaden gritted his teeth, and his hand dug into her mane. With ease, he directed her and Claudia never gagged once. Her fierce but tender assault had him marveling at her hastiness. And her mouth rained a warm wetness that made him growl like an estranged animal.

Claudia was enjoying her meal, and she wondered why it had taken her so long to make it to this portion of dinner.

"Mmmmm," she moaned, sliding her tongue on the firm, slickness of his bone. Her momentum sped up, and more moans left her.

"Fuck!" Jaden swore. He threw his head back his jaw locking. Claudia sucked him whole, and Jaden's orgasm fled through his shaft. He attempted to pull away, but Claudia held firm refusing to allow him the bereft he hadn't given her.

"Chérie, if you don't stop I'm going to..." Claudia sucked him deeper, harder, holding him stronger. Jaden could wait no longer. Claudia set off an explosion that coated her mouth in layers.

"Fuuuuccck!" he yelled stumbling backward. But Claudia was right with him, moving her jaws until he'd weakened and fell to one knee effectively pulling his dick from her mouth. Finally, she moved, her eyes soaking him up.

He took in a deep breath, his gaze now wildly untamed. "That's how you want to play it, huh?"

Jaden reached down and grabbed her roughly, hauling Claudia against a wall pinning her there with his abdomen. Claudia's heart slammed as he took in her mouth, his hands discovering her all over again. They made love and enjoyed rough nefarious sex for the duration of the day going from one landing to the other. They'd become completely undone, and with each time they came together, their experience heightened into unknown territories.

They did take a moment to eat and even have light conversation. But for the length of time spent in the room together, their mouths were busy exploring other intricate details that left them both spent.

Chapter Nineteen

Over the next few days, Claudia and Jaden had their hands full of each other. Literally, going from one tantalizing show to another. On the gondola ride at the Venetian Shoppes, Claudia had once again fallen asleep in Jaden's arms. She'd seen ten minutes of the scenery before her eyes closed and she was off in dreamland.

When it was over, Jaden woke her with a smooth kiss to her lips. Claudia had never felt better. Minutes later, they made it to The Dream live show. Claudia was in awe of the talented actors. They'd put on a wistful presentation of choreography with fire and ice, high dives, and underwater tangos. That part specifically had drawn in Claudia's attention, and she'd caught Jaden staring at her with a smirk and a wink.

"I know those hips of yours can tango like that," he'd whispered in her ear. "I've seen first-hand so don't you dare deny it."

Claudia giggled to the moon and back and Jaden had sent nibbles down her earlobe and neck. He was driving her insane and every moment being with him was like living a dream.

Their days had been filled with so much sexual chemistry and fun, sometimes they forgot to eat. As they lay on the blanket stretched across the green grass at Spring Mountain Ranch State Park, the stars shone brightly overhead. Claudia took up space in the place she'd come to love which was right on Jaden's chest. Reaching over, she plucked a grape out of the bowl she'd packed for their picnic, and turned to lean into him, feeding Jaden the sweet treat. With pleasure, Jaden opened to receive the fruit.

"This could be my life," he said.

"What, me feeding you grapes?"

"Yes ma'am," he said.

Claudia snickered. "Mine, too."

She rolled back to her back and sighed, knowing their time in Vegas had come to an end. Tomorrow morning, they were set to go back to the reality of Chicago, where her business, and family awaited. It wasn't as if she didn't want to get back to those things. She did, but there was always something that needed immediate attention, especially the benefit she was putting together.

"What's on your mind, chérie?"

Claudia glanced at him then back to the starlit sky. "I went to the bank for a loan for my benefit I'm putting together."

"Oh yeah, how'd that go?"

"They denied me."

Jaden frowned. "What was their reason for denying you?"

"It seems I don't have the assets to gain a substantial loan from them. However, they told me I could use my part of S&M financial advisory as collateral, but I would never do that. So, they told me I was on my own. It's a real shame, too. There are so many caregivers in the city of Chicago alone that go without the resources they need."

Claudia frowned. "I almost told the bank manager to kiss my ass."

This brought on a heavy chortle from Jaden. Claudia looked at him. "I did." She shrugged.

"Don't worry about it, chérie, I'd be more than happy to help you out."

Claudia's eyes bugged, and she rose to her elbows. "How could you? You don't even know how much I need to make this thing come to fruition."

"Whatever it is, I've got you."

"Why because I put it on you like this?" Claudia did a little wiggle with her hips.

Jaden rolled to the side and howled. Claudia laughed as she continued to shake her hips. Jaden's laughter slowly subsided, and he threw his arms around her.

"That's not the reason," he said with humor still in his voice.

"Mmhmm, then what's the reason?"

Jaden's hold tightened. "Because you're a beautiful person. Here..." he pointed to her heart. "Inside and out. I've watched you handle your business, care for your mother, help out others, all while neglecting yourself. Even now, this benefit you're putting together is selfless.

So I'm taking a page from your book. My selfless act, giving you the funds needed to secure the spot for your benefit and anything else. I also have a few clients to reach out to that wouldn't mind donating. It would be my honor to help you, chérie. If you'll allow it."

"Under one condition," she said giggling at the wry look on his face. "You'll let me pay you back."

"No."

Claudia gasped. "What do you mean no? That's the terms or all bets are off."

Jaden held her with a pensive stare.

"What?" she said.

"You're not paying me back, AND, you're taking my money. Now hush woman. I'll hear nothing else about it."

"I don't feel comfortable taking your money, Jaden."

Jaden was almost at a loss for words. "I think that's the first time I've heard that coming from a woman."

Claudia snickered. "Well I'm sure I'm not the type of woman you're accustomed to."

That much was true, he thought.

"I can't take your money. We're friends, and friends pay each other back."

"What if we were more than friends, then would you need to pay me back?"

Claudia peered at him her heart racing. "We're not, so what's the point in imagining?"

"Chérie," Jaden gave her complete eye contact. "We are more than friends."

Claudia's gaze fell from his eyes to his moist lips and back up again.

"I'm making you my girlfriend. Now you can't give the money back."

Claudia gasped a sultry laughing escaping her. "Excuse me," she feigned offense. "You can't just make me your girlfriend. You have to ask, and besides, who says I'm not seeing someone already?"

Jaden's jaw clenched, and his pupils darkened. Surely, she wouldn't be in a relationship with someone the way they'd made love the last few days. Images of Claudia with someone else attacked Jaden's mind and steam poured from his ears. Claudia watched him intently, and if she didn't know any better, she would've sworn she'd seen him transform right in front of her eyes.

"Baby..."

"Are you seeing anyone, Claudia?"

A few seconds ticked by. "I have other male friends, but no, I'm not seeing anyone exclusively."

"We'll you are now, and we'll make sure to get rid of those friends."

Claudia's eyes widened, at the same time her heart soared. Before she could respond Jaden spoke again. "Will you be my girlfriend, Claudia?"

Claudia folded her arms regardless of the fact she was secretly in love with him. She needed to put up a tough front. If there was anything she learned growing up in Chicago, it was not to give in too quickly.

"You look like you want to put up a fight," Jaden said. "Maybe I should rephrase my words. Would you be interested in being in a relationship with me, chérie?"

Claudia's heart warmed, and she forced herself not to shout hell yeah. Instead, she thought about her life and still considered herself a nobody when compared to the women he'd dated before.

"Are you serious?"

"Of course, I am." He pulled her closer. "I want to be with you. Tell me you want to be with me, too."

Claudia was apprehensive. Things like this didn't happen to her. She wasn't the girl that got the guy at the end of the day. She held back from pinching herself to save herself the embarrassment.

Her unresponsiveness twisted Jaden's gut. "There's someone else, isn't there?"

"No," she quickly spoke up. "It's not that."

"Then what is it?"

A smile crossed her lips, "Nothing," she dipped her head low then looked back into his eyes. "I'd love to be your," she paused, "girlfriend, Jaden."

His eyes twinkled, and a smile laced with mischief graced his masculine face. "You know what that means, don't you?"

"No, what?"

"We have to celebrate." He drew her in. His gruff voice whispered, "All... night... long..."

When Jaden and Claudia made it back to Chicago, Claudia had him drop her off at S&M Financial Advisory.

"Can I bother you for lunch?" he asked.

"Of course."

Jaden leaned in for a kiss and Claudia met him halfway.

"Your lips are always a delicious treat for me," he said.

Claudia blushed. "That's good to know," she winked.

His cell phone buzzed, and they both glanced down to the middle console where it sat. Cassie's face covered the screen, and Jaden silenced the phone.

"Do you need to get that?"

"It's not important."

"Okay, I'll see you at one, then."

Jaden exited his vehicle, and Claudia watched his long strides carry him around to the passenger door. Upon opening, he held out his hand, and she delightfully took it. "I'll see you at one, chérie."

He left a kiss on her cheek and waited until she disappeared inside the building before reclaiming his seat and pulling away.

Claudia was on cloud nine. She pretty much skipped her way inside the building. The way she was feeling, Claudia could've taken the stairs two at a time. But she waited patiently with a smile on her face for the elevator doors to open.

It was nine a.m., and Claudia had gotten a little nap on their flight from Vegas to Chicago. When the doors opened, she stepped in.

"Hold the doors, please!"

Octavia ran down the hallway and glided into the elevator just as the doors shut. "Right on time," Claudia said.

Octavia blew out a breath. "Barely. It seemed as if it was one thing after another this morning."

"What happened?"

"For starters, my toilet clogged and it wasn't something I could fix with a simple plunger. I had to call a plumber. What's worst is, you know that early morning pee is a must, girl I had to run to my neighbor's house. You should've seen the way she scowled at me when I asked to use her bathroom. Like I'd woke her up... standing there with rollers in her head and a crooked nightgown. Maybe if she got a job like regular folks, she wouldn't be so bothered with getting up so early."

Claudia laughed.

"I'm standing there bouncing up and down. Damn near had piss running down my leg."

"Oh my God! That's too much information!"

"Well," Octavia said shrugging, "It might be, but I had to give you that tidbit so you could feel my whole story."

The elevator doors dinged and parted. The ladies strutted into the office building headed straight for the café machine.

"That ain't even the half of it; then my car didn't start," Octavia shook her head. "I had to take an Uber to work. That's why I'm running through the doors late."

"Hey, I know something about that," Claudia added. "My car is in the shop right now, but I need to go pick it up. Should be fixed by now, but the mechanic hasn't called."

"Maybe someone could call if you'd had your phone on," came a voice behind Claudia.

A smile fell across her face as she turned to Samiyah.

"But I'm not mad at you though, we all can't be out falling in love like somebody I know."

Claudia tossed her head back and laughed. "Maybe that's because you've already done that."

Samiyah pursed her lips with hands on her hips. "Okay, you got me there."

"Un huh, I know I do!"

The girls laughed.

"So that's where you've been," Octavia swooned.

"I don't know what you're talking about." Claudia sipped her café.

"Right, I don't know why you insist on keeping your adventures with prince charming to yourself."

Claudia smirked. "Some things a girl must hold on to."

Samiyah was shaking her head. "Don't even think about it."

"What?"

"You know what, spill it!"

Chapter Twenty

Jonas bent forward and stretched, then pulled himself upright to jog in place. He looked to his stopwatch and set the timer when someone approached. Glancing over, a broad smile spread across his face.

"That was quite a disappearing act you did little brother and out of character might I add. What's up with you?"

Jaden slapped hands with his brother and pulled him in for a man hug. The men were dressed down in their running gear, with shorts that hung to their knees, a thin t-shirt that framed their muscled physiques, and running shoes.

"I should've known I wouldn't be able to slide that by you."

"You got that right. Besides you forget, my wife is best friends with your... hmmm, what shall I call her little brother?"

Jaden's smile was wide. "Her name is Claudia."

Jonas laughed. "Yeah, that much I'm aware of. But what's she to you?"

Jaden waited a beat before responding. "I told her she was my girlfriend."

"You told her?"

"Hell yeah."

Jonas threw his head back and howled. Jaden's smile spread even further.

"You won't be the only one around here getting some action."

Jonas agreed, shaking his head up and down. "So that's all it is then, you getting some action?"

"Nah, you know what I mean."

"Yeah," Jonas rubbed his chin. "I think I do."

"Oh, I'm sure you do."

"I'm happy for you man. There's a first time for everything."

Jaden frowned. "You act as if I've never dated before man, please."

"Yeah, you've dated, but you've never singled out one woman over another."

Jaden went to object but thought about Jonas' words. It was true. He'd dated many women, but the last time he held a serious relationship, if you could even call it that, was in high school. And if Jaden was real with himself, no one was ever serious in high school.

"You're right, and if I feel anything like you feel about Samiyah, then I think I might be in trouble."

Jonas' eyes widened. "Hold up, are you saying you're in love with the girl?"

"Claudia," Jaden reiterated. "Her name is Claudia."

Jonas held his hands up in surrender. "My bad, you're right, Claudia." A broad smile covered Jonas' lips. "Well I'll be damned; my little brother is in love."

Jaden didn't reply. It had crossed his mind many times over the last few days, but hearing Jonas say it made it that much more authentic and he couldn't deny it.

"Listen, let's get through this run. I've got a few conference calls today that may take up most of my time, and I have other things on the agenda."

"Let me guess. Those other things have to do with Claudia?"

Jaden smiled wide and winked. "Let's go sucka," he said taking off in a sprint.

After taking a quick shower and heading to the office, Jaden's cell phone rang. Again, it was Cassie. Jaden thought about not answering then decided against it. If the call were personal, he'd politely tell her he wasn't interested.

"What can I do you for Ms. Singapore," his smooth voice seeped through the phone.

"Are we formal now Jaden? Should I call you, Mr. Rose?"

"Nah, Jaden's fine. What's up?"

"I wanted to talk with you about something important. Is your lunch schedule free?"

"Actually, it's not. Why don't you tell me what it's about while you have me on the phone?"

Cassie hesitated. "I want to invest in your hedge fund, and I've been reading some material on how to go about doing that. I figured since you're the man with the master plan, you can assist me."

Jaden thought about Claudia. He didn't want to cancel his lunch date with her, but being that this was a business call, he would need to. He slid his tongue across his teeth and thought about it a bit more. Jaden knew he had to be careful with Cassie. She was interested in more than investments, but she had donated to his mother's charity for the last five years.

"Meet me at Jasper's at one. We'll talk about it then," Jaden acquiesced.

"Great, I look forward to it. See you soon."

Jaden disconnected the call and pulled into Rose Bank and Trust Credit Union. Before going inside, he dialed Claudia's number and waited patiently for her to answer. Her cell rang three times before going to voicemail. Jaden disconnected. She must have been busy. He opened his messages and sent, her a text.

Chérie, unfortunately, I need to cancel our lunch date. It looks like I'll be working throughout the day. When you get a chance call me back.

Jaden dropped the phone in his pocket and exited the vehicle with thoughts of Claudia dancing around his head.

Lunch time didn't come soon enough. Jaden had three conference calls today and the first one lasted most of his morning. He pulled out his cell feeling a bit disappointed with no missed calls or text messages from Claudia. Her day must be just as busy as his. Revving his engine, Jaden pulled out of the parking lot heading for Jasper's. Besides Chicago being its usual windy day, the sun sat high and suddenly, Jaden wished he was in his drop top.

It was a good day to let the top down and ride with the wind breezing about. His mind went to Claudia and what her hair would look like flowing in the wind.

"You've got it bad son," he spoke to himself. "Especially now that you're driving down the street, talking to yourself." Jaden grinned and shook his head. He was tempted to blow off the meeting with Cassie and pop in on Claudia. If she hadn't gotten his message, she would think he'd stood her up. Jaden went to call her again but decided against it. If she was truly busy, he didn't want to disturb her.

"It's no problem at all Mr. Ralphshire, thank you for your business."

Claudia shook the older gentleman's hand, and he left her office. She blew out a heavy sighed and strolled back to her desk. Because her schedule was made weeks in advance, sometimes Claudia would forget when she was double-booked. She took a glance at the time; it was 1:45 pm. She'd skipped out on lunch since Jaden had other plans come up. It was too bad because she was looking forward to seeing him again. A small smile flickered across her lips. Every time Claudia had a free moment, her thoughts would venture to Jaden.

She pulled her cell phone out and sent him a text;

Hey you, it seems we both have a busy day ahead of us. Maybe we can get lunch tomorrow? Call me when you get a chance.

There was a knock at her door, and Claudia turned her attention to it.

"You getting lunch?" Octavia asked, peeking her head in the door.

"I should since I haven't had anything."

"I'm going to the grill downstairs you're more than welcomed to join me."

Claudia rose to her feet and grabbed her purse. "I couldn't refuse if I wanted to. My stomach would surely be upset with me."

Octavia laughed, and they left the office.

"We probably should've asked Samiyah if she wanted anything."

Claudia side eyed her. "Girl if you think Samiyah is in that office during lunch time you're crazy. She has her hands full with Jonas."

"Her door was closed, and I heard voices," Octavia said perplexed.

"That means Jonas is inside and trust me you don't want to disturb them."

Octavia crinkled her nose. "Ew, I've sat in those chairs in her office and that sofa."

"The seats may be safe, but the sofa..." Claudia tilted her head as if to say, 'I can't help you there.'

"Wow."

"Oh, girl when you get a hunk of a man, trust me, he'll have you upside down in your office, too. Just make sure it's lunch time and were closed."

Octavia gasped her hand flying over her chest. Claudia waved her off. "Don't be such a prude; you know you'd like it."

Octavia opened her mouth then closed it.

"That's what I thought," Claudia said.

Later that night Claudia stretched out in her bed. One leg was thrown off the side. It was after midnight, and she hadn't heard a peep from Jaden. Unfortunately for her, thoughts of him were perpetual, and she'd wondered about his whereabouts all day. Every time she went to call she would back out, reasoning that if he could spare the time, he'd call. Right?

But the incessant voice in the back of her head reminded Claudia of Jaden's lifestyle and his promiscuous ways. She'd waved the thoughts off, but they would come back to haunt her the longer the day went on with no sign of him. They had a wonderful weekend in Vegas and going into it, Claudia told herself not to get wrapped up in his charm. But, Claudia did, and she hoped it wasn't a mistake.

"I'm bugging," she said to herself, "It hasn't even been twenty-four hours. A dry laugh left her, and she was determined to put her mind to rest and sleep, but she continued to toss and turn throughout the night with sleep evading her.

The next day, Claudia received an email from the Mayor of Chicago. At first glance, she thought it was a mistake, but a closer look at the correspondence revealed it was truly the Mayor with his official logo attached at the bottom. It appeared he received some information about her nonprofit organization and wanted to attend her benefit with a few friends. Claudia's eyes widened. There was no way he'd found out about Caregivers Organization through her efforts. Claudia knew her reach didn't range that far. But Jaden? That was an entirely different story in itself.

"Of course," she'd said to herself as she squealed.

Having the mayor attend her event with a few friends could mean one thousand people give or take. This was big news. Claudia squealed again and hit reply just as her phone rang. Jaden was calling.

"Good morning." The smile on her face could be heard in her voice.

"The morning would've been better with you by my side. But I'll take what I can get, for now."

Claudia's smile grew brighter. All those thoughts that haunted her last night went out the window.

"I missed you yesterday," she said trying not to sound too desperate.

"Did you?"

Claudia scoffed and rolled her eyes. "Of course."

Jaden chuckled. "I missed you as well, chérie."

Claudia's stomach was in knots. Just the sound of his warm, inviting voice would soak her panties. It was amazing that he didn't even have to try to get her wound up.

"Did you get my text message yesterday afternoon?"

"I did, and unfortunately, I was on my phone most of the day with one conference call after another."

Claudia understood. Jaden worked with investments and people always needed to be reassured that their money was in the right hands.

"Well, what do you think about lunch, today?"

"I'm game if you are."

"How about I pick you up for lunch," Claudia said.

A deep laugh rumbled from him. "I don't think so. What kind of man do you take me for?"

"The traditional one, it seems."

"You would be right, chérie. I'll pick you up."

"Fine, I guess."

Jaden chuckled.

"Oh, I received, an email from the Mayor and I'd just like to say, Oh, my God and thank you very much."

"I can't take the credit," he said.

Claudia frowned. "What do you mean?"

"I had nothing to do with the Mayor contacting you. Is it about your Caregivers Organization?"

"Yes."

"Well if you've received the attention of the mayor, you're doing something right."

Claudia was in shock, her mouth hanging wide open, but then she pursed her lips. Jaden was lying to her.

There was no way he didn't have anything to do with the mayor contacting her, but if he wanted to pretend like she'd pulled this correspondence off by herself, she'd let him.

Jaden's phone beeped, and he glanced at his screen.

"Sweetheart I need to take this other line, do you mind?"

"No not at all, handle your business, and I'll wait for more info about lunch."

"I'll get back to you soon."

They disconnected the call, and Claudia sat; still over the moon. Throughout the day she'd made calls to hire caterers, interior designers and party planners for her upcoming event. It was last minute considering she'd set the date of the benefit three months away. Nobody puts together an event that fast, Samiyah had told her, but Claudia would. For years now Claudia had had the idea floating around her brain. It was an intensive outline that she added to up until today. All she needed to do was execute it and with Jaden on her side and now the Mayor, Claudia could pull off this gathering in weeks if need be.

When an email came through from Jaden's assistant asking for her bank account info, Claudia froze. She sent Jaden a text to confirm it was him and he shot back a quick text explaining that he needed an account to send over funds that would go towards her benefit. Breathing a sigh of relief, Claudia sent the information over to his assistant and thanked him but not without telling Jaden she was still paying him back.

I don't think so. Jaden had responded, and Claudia had only giggled and rolled her eyes.

When lunch time came, she sat composed and ready for their time together but again, Jaden was a no show. This time, she didn't even receive a text message or a phone call. The hour passed and Claudia reasoned that he must've gotten caught up at work again. She left the office deciding to pick up something quick from the sandwich shop across the street. She entered and placed her order, but on the way to the pickup line, Claudia did a double take, reaching down to remove a newspaper from a nearby stand. A picture of Jaden coming out of Jasper's restaurant with Cassie was splashed across the front. The headline read;

Jaden Alexander Rose with a new love interest?

Claudia's stomach churned, her immediate response a punitive oath. Her eyes roamed across the words as the article deliberated about the mystery woman he'd been seen with the week before. In the photo, Jaden was helping Cassie Singapore, Owner of Dance Studios into the passenger seat of his Lexus and Cassie was staring at him with dreamy eyes. Anger flared in Claudia before she caught herself. But then she remembered where she was. Claudia put the paper back in its stand and went out the door; her sandwich all but forgotten.

Outside she took a deep breath as a thousand thoughts poured through her. Wasn't Claudia his girlfriend? They made that official before returning to Chicago. So why was she feeling played already? Claudia crossed the street, and a horn blew forcing her to take a step back.

"Focus," she said needing to make it across the street in one piece.

Back inside her building, Claudia held up against a wall needing to calm herself. Why would Jaden pretend he was working all day when clearly he had other intentions? Didn't he know his popularity in the city made it impossible to pull off such a thing?

"Calm down," Claudia spoke to herself, "looks can be deceiving, I'm sure whatever was going on, there is a good reason for it."

Claudia wanted to believe it, but leaving out any mention of a lunch date with Cassie didn't sit well with her. In the back of Claudia's mind, she knew Jaden was most likely exercising his playboy ways. Claudia sighed and went back to her office; her day all but ruined.

Chapter Twenty One

Two weeks passed with minimal conversation with Jaden. The three times, Claudia had been in his presence he'd seemed withdrawn and unfocused. She couldn't have been imagining it. Besides that, their conversations were almost obsolete. With the way Jaden was working, he would never have time for a serious relationship, and she pondered why he even tried it with her.

Claudia wanted to reach out to him, ask if everything was okay or if he needed time alone to focus on his career. But every time she encouraged herself, her fingers would hover over his name, and she would never hit send. Who was she kidding? Of course, Claudia wanted to continue seeing him, but that was becoming scarce. Thoughts of her father leaving their family when she was just a young teenager ballooned. Claudia hadn't been awake for five minutes the morning he'd kissed her on the temples and promised to see her later.

But he never came home. Just like that, her father disappeared without a trace, and she didn't even know if he was still alive today. Claudia fidgeted behind her computer screen determined to get some work done, but her attention was elsewhere, so there was no use. Giving up, Claudia left her office deciding to cut her losses and head home early. On her drive, Claudia's cell rang, and Jaden's handsome face eased across the screen. Claudia went to answer but held back. Maybe she should end things with him.

Going on with Jaden the way things were now was throwing Claudia off her game. Lately, she'd been robotic when talking to her mother. Besides helping Adeline getting in and out of bed, Claudia was around only long enough to make sure Adeline took her medicine then Claudia was gone. At work, Claudia had been so distracted during a phone call with a client that she'd had to replay their recorded call to find out what she was supposed to be helping him with.

Claudia's phone stopped ringing and a few seconds later a text message came through.

Missing you.

Claudia's heart melted. She missed Jaden with a passion, and that was the problem. Images of his smooth-shaven face and sexy suckable lips came to her. She sighed blowing out a deep breath, and pulled into her driveway shutting off the engine. Claudia pondered on whether to return his call or text. She did neither opting to let bygones be bygones.

More weeks went by with Claudia ducking and dodging Jaden's phone calls. There weren't many of them, but when they came in, her nerves would stand on edge, and she'd talk herself into not answering.

"You're a strong woman. You don't need a man to complete you. Don't let him break through. You've got this. Just let it go. Move on."

This was her daily mantra depending on how many times Jaden called her in a day. However, Claudia had thrown herself into work. Coming in as early as six in the morning and leaving as late as eight o'clock at night. She'd taken her sister's advice and hired a part time caregiver for Adeline since Claudia wasn't there most of the time.

Stepping over the threshold of their home, Claudia could smell food cooking. Lifting her nose to the air, Claudia frowned. She knew Adeline wasn't cooking this late, so who was? Making her way around the corner to the kitchen came with a surprising sight. London, her part time caregiver, stood next to the counter, and Adeline sat across from her. Both of them watched Jaden as he chopped vegetables like a skilled chef. Whatever he was cooking smelled delightful and it reminded Claudia that she hadn't eaten since lunch.

Lingering in the doorway, watching them, felt like invading on their personal lives. They appeared to be a mini family with Adeline gushing at Jaden's fast chopping skills and London smitten with his charm. Claudia rolled her eyes. Who could blame the girl? Jaden had that effect on most women. It didn't take longer than thirty seconds before he glanced up, his eyes meeting hers. A smile spread across his lips.

"Good evening, chérie." He glanced over at the clock on the wall noting the late time. "Long day at the office?"

Everyone turned to Claudia.

"Ms. Stevens," London said traipsing over to her. "I hope you don't mind, Jaden wanted to wait for you about something important, so I figured..."

"That you'd let a complete stranger into my house?"

Jaden bristled, and his jaw clenched.

"Your house?" Adeline squawked. "I thought this was our home and I let Jaden in, not London. He's no stranger, what's gotten into you?"

"He's a stranger to London, and since she's in charge when I'm not here, then she's responsible for letting him in."

"You're right, I apologize. I didn't think you would have a problem with it," London said.

"Why?"

London blubbered out a response. "Well, at first I was going to tell him, no, but Adeline said it was okay, so..."

"Get your things. Your service is no longer needed here."

London gasped.

"Claudia!" Adeline screeched.

"Leave now," Claudia continued.

"Yes, ma'am." London flew past Claudia in a rush to relieve herself from the embarrassment she felt.

"You can't do that! She didn't do anything wrong!" Adeline fussed.

"I just did."

"You know your attitude lately has been pretty nasty. What? Are you on your period or something!?!"

Enough

Jaden laid a gentle hand on Adeline's shoulder and removed his apron. Adeline set her sights on him just as she went to fuss at Claudia more.

"Let me talk to her."

Adeline huffed, pulling herself to her feet and grabbing her walker. She trudged past Claudia with a glare on her face mumbling underneath her breath. When Jaden and Claudia were the only ones in the room, his penetrating gaze soaked her up. Claudia, determined to be strong, didn't squirm visibly under his intense scrutiny, willing herself to hold firm.

"I seem to have upset you unwillingly."

He took a few steps toward her and Claudia wanted like all hell to retreat. But she held steady and said nothing. With him standing mere inches in front of her, Jaden went on. "You don't have to fire London, she's good with Adeline, and Adeline likes her company." He reached out to Claudia, and she flinched.

"How would you know? Are you and London involved, too?"

Jaden's brows furrowed. "Involved, too?"

He rubbed his chin; a questionable look on his face.

"I don't know her, but I've seen her with your mom tonight, and they get along well." He reached out for her again, and this time she allowed him to pull her in. "The only person I'm supposed to be involved with, is you, chérie. But lately I'm not sure if that's the case since you've been ignoring my calls." He held her with a steady gaze. "What's going on? Talk to me."

Claudia was losing her resolve, and she needed to get his hands off of her before he could melt the iceberg that stood in front of them.

"You should cut your losses now, Jaden. There's no need for you to stick around and pretend you're interested in dating me. I'm giving you an out. Now, you and Cassie can date without me finding out through paparazzi." She took a step out of his arms.

Jaden's brows rose, and he cursed. "It's not what it looks like. Paparazzi take pictures of me with anyone."

"Then they must be selective because I've only seen you and her in the newspaper, coming out of Jaspers when we were supposed to have a lunch date. Then there was that picture of you two at the studio dancing in front of a crowd. I think the headline said," Claudia held her head in thought, "Oh yes," she snapped her fingers, "Love on the horizon. That's it. Not to mention one of you leaving her home after you'd told me you'd had a long day."

"You have valid points. If you'll just let me explain."

Claudia waved him off. "I don't need an explanation. I get it. Relationships aren't your thing, so I'll let you off the hook. At this point in my life, it doesn't matter. It seems every man I've ever loved abandons me anyway. Why would you be any different?"

A fresh mist of tears blurred Claudia's vision, and she backed away, fleeing down the hall desperately trying to get away from him. When she stepped inside her room, immediately she realized her mistake.

Strong arms enveloped her as a sob escaped her throat. Damn, she didn't want to cry in front of him. The last thing she wanted was him feeling sorry for her. His lips found her ears, and he spoke.

"There is no way I'm letting you run away from this relationship. I am not seeing Cassie. She is a client. Me being at her studio had everything to do with helping the neighborhood kids and nothing to do with a romantic involvement with her. I would never cheat on my woman. You have to believe me."

Claudia fought to get away from him, denying herself the reassurance that he gave. Jaden knew the subject of Cassie was an issue and he was sure Claudia's comment about men she loved abandoning her was more so about her father. He felt entirely responsible for not digging into the conversation sooner, and he hated to know her tears stemmed from something he'd done.

"I can't do this, Jaden," Claudia whispered hoarsely.

"Yes, you can." He turned her to face him. "You love me?"

Claudia's tear stained eyes widen. "Wha-what?

"You said, the men that you love... Do you love me, Claudia?"

Claudia's heart melted. She had slipped and said that.

"Forget I said it, I didn't mean... I..."

"You didn't mean it?"

Claudia darted her attention away from him, "Jaden, please just go."

"I'm not going anywhere. You know why? Because I've done nothing wrong. So, we've gone days without seeing each other. Sometimes both of our schedules are busy, but I'm with you. No one else. I don't want to be with anyone else. I can change my schedule, it's not a problem, and I won't see Cassie anymore. It is my fault for letting things get as bad as they have and for that, I apologize."

He placed a soft kiss on her face, nose, and closed eyelids. Claudia thawed under his warmth. "I can't, Jaden." She shook her head as sadness weighed her down. "I'm no good for you or anyone else. I'm damaged beyond repair. I won't stop you from going about your life. I'm sorry we ever got involved."

Jaden's jaw tightened. "You don't mean that."

Claudia shook her head vehemently. "Yes I do." She struggled to get out of his arms.

"Claudia," he said holding on to her as if his life depended on it.

"Let me go, Jaden."

"Claudia!"

She pushed herself through his barrier, and he released her. Her feet back pedaled, and he stalked her with each step she took. When her back hit the wall next to a dresser she held her arms out to stop his advancement.

"Claudia..."

"Please, Jaden, just go. It was fun while it lasted, right? Maybe sometime in the future, we can be friends."

Jaden's gaze flowed over her as he stood there brooding. Frustration and agitation rolled off him in waves. Suddenly, he moved, so fast that Claudia didn't have a chance to fight him before his mouth liquefied into hers. With his hands, Jaden gripped her shirt and sank his fingers into her waist molding her frame against his massive chest. He spread her lips apart with his tongue and invaded her hot wet mouth. An inferno covered Claudia from head to toe, and she moaned against his lips.

Desire hummed through Jaden, and his manhood bobbled against her throbbing sex. The flavor of his mouth caused Claudia to suck his tongue, and Jaden ripped her blouse to shreds causing her body to jerk against the wall. A tremble vibrated down her skin as Jaden's kiss led a blaze of heat down her throat to her rock-hard nipples. He sucked in one of the beautiful brown areolas and Claudia sucked in a breath. Removing her skintight bottoms would've proved difficult from an inexperienced lover, but Jaden had no problem where that area was concerned, as he forcefully drug the pants off and tossed them to the side. With his mouth, Jaden placed passionate kisses up her legs to her thighs, the vibration from Claudia's body unmistaken as his lips landed on every part of her.

Claudia fought to gain some sense of control, but she was beyond sanity. When Jaden's tongue lapped at her clitoris, a whimper fell from her mouth, and she dropped. Jaden's arms clasped a stronghold on her, and he rose to his feet lifting her off the ground with ease. Claudia's legs wrapped around his waist while Jaden simultaneously unzipped his pants with his other hand and plunged inside of her.

"Aaaaah!" Claudia yelled.

"Does this feel like we can be friends, Claudia?"

Burying himself within her, Claudia's mouth fell open, and with his mouth, he took her lips in whole. They dissolved into one another as his powerful thrust tore into her desperately.

They knocked against the wall and Claudia's screams were swallowed by his masterful tongue. Claudia's heart thundered as Jaden slapped against her walls trying with pleasure to disassemble the barricade she refused to take down.

"We can't be friends, chérie," he growled against her mouth. "I don't fuck my friends this way."

She whimpered again; her eyes rolling into the back of her head.

"I won't be reduced to a friend. I don't want to be your friend. I want to be your man." A torched burned through his veins as he made his declarations and his distributed unlawful agility to his thrusts that sent an orgasm ripping through them both. Thoughtfully, Jaden kept her mouth covered with his to drown out her moans as they both soared to a new height of desire.

Claudia's heart rammed against her chest, and her head rolled seconds before she passed out. With her slumped forward in his arms Jaden walked them to her bed and laid her down. Alarmed, he placed two fingers over her neck to feel for a pulse. It thumped strong against his fingers and Jaden blew out a breath. Slowly, he removed himself from her.

Shit, he thought. They hadn't used a condom. In his haste to be inside of her, he'd foolishly forgotten to put one on. His gaze darted to her belly, and he imagined it swollen with his babies. A smile tugged at the corner of his mouth and a comfortable heat passed over him. Crawling onto the bed, Jaden pulled Claudia against him and held her thinking about the words she'd spoken.

Jaden had gone about this relationship all wrong. Instead of putting Claudia first, he'd put her last allowing his career to come before her. The days and nights he hadn't spoken with her had been painfully lonely. And Jaden never thought he'd ever feel that way. Women he'd dealt with in the past called and stopped by his condo more often than he cared to admit, but turning them away was easy when before he'd given them admittance. In truth, Jaden had been a loyal boyfriend but not a very good one. He vowed to rectify that.

Claudia was who he desired more than he'd ever needed anyone. He didn't even get a chance to tell her the real reason he was pictured leaving Cassie's house. Cassie knew how to pull Jaden's heart strings. She'd called him with alarm in her voice saying her son was having a seizure and she needed a ride to the hospital. By the time he'd arrived, her son was fine sitting on the couch drinking a glass of water. When he questioned her, she told him it wasn't as bad as she'd initially thought; apologizing profusely about interrupting his night.

Jaden wanted to give her the benefit of the doubt. Surely, Cassie wouldn't use her son as a scapegoat to get to him. But none of that mattered now. If Cassie wanted to keep her funds invested in Rose Bank and Trust, he'd give her account to someone else. He wouldn't risk losing Claudia again. Jaden laid with his thoughts for the better part of an hour before he drifted off to sleep. When he rose, it was 5 am, and he needed to get his day started. Quietly Jaden pulled his arms away from up under Claudia and eased out of bed. His eyes fell on her tempting body, and his manhood sprang to life.

"Down boy," he whispered, "unfortunately, we'll have to take a raincheck."

He walked through the house quietly like a ghost disappearing within seconds.

Chapter Twenty Two

A soft hand grazed Claudia's face rocking her gently. Opening her eyes, Claudia squinted and smiled at her mother.

"Good morning baby," Adeline said. "Are you taking the day off?"

Claudia's eyes widened as she propped herself up on her elbows.

"What time is it?"

"9:40."

Claudia groaned and rolled to her back with arms splayed at her sides. Last night she'd had a blissful dream about Jaden rocking her world and apparently it had made her oversleep. Just after having that thought the ache between Claudia's thighs told her otherwise. Pulling back to her elbows Claudia glanced at her mother. Had she heard her and Jaden last night? Memories of her wails and yelps came slamming to the forefront.

"I didn't see Jaden leave. I guess you two kissed and made up?"

A flush of embarrassment fell over Claudia, and she rolled her face back into the pillows with another groan.

It was then that she realized her bottom was bare. Frantically, Claudia reached down and pulled the covers over her nakedness.

"Too late for that, I used to wipe that little butt remember."

Claudia groaned again. "Ma!"

"Well, I did."

"Do you mind leaving the room so I can get myself together, please?"

"As soon as you get on the phone and rehire London."

London. Claudia remembered firing her. Claudia had been so upset and disappointed with herself for letting Jaden get up under her skin that she'd fired London for letting him in. Jaden. There was no way she could get him out of her heart within a few days or even weeks. Last night, he'd spoken like she meant everything to him, but she told the truth about her current status. Claudia was damaged goods. And she didn't want to bring a man down who had his stuff together.

"I'll call London when I get to my office, but I'm already late. Now can you please step out so I can change?"

Adeline was good for putting up a fight, but this morning she didn't feel like it. "Don't come home without calling her."

"Excuse me?"

"You heard me," Adeline wiggled her butt off the bed, bracing her weight on the walker.

After she left, Claudia scurried out of bed and shut the door turning her back against it.

"Get it together girl, you've got a busy day."

Claudia went about the business of showering, moisturizing and dressing. She pulled her hair off her face today and paid extra attention to applying her foundation. When she stepped in S & M Financial Advisory, Samiyah, Octavia, and Selena all had clients in their offices, which was fine by Claudia since she didn't feel like talking anyway. She was still trying to sort out what she should do about Jaden.

Closing her door, Claudia rounded the desk. She hit the speaker and dialed a number.

"Ms. Stevens?"

"Good morning, London." Claudia paused. "Listen, last night I was tired and upset. There was no reason for my behavior. I need you. Can you pick up where you left off?"

Claudia heard a sigh on the other line. "Of course, I am terribly sorry. You won't have to worry about me doing that again."

"Well, that's good to hear. I'll try not to overreact like that again."

"Thank you, Ms. Stevens."

"Just call me Claudia. We're both around the same age, there's no need for the formality."

"Alright, I'll head over there now."

"Thanks, have a good day, bye now."

Claudia disconnected the line and sat down in her seat. Her benefit was a couple of weeks away, and her nerves were frazzled about how well it would go. Would she meet the goals she set? Five hundred thousand dollars is what she wanted to raise. But was it too much? Claudia rested against her chair and twirled in the swivel seat.

Her cell rang that familiar tune and where she wanted to smile and be complaisant, she felt obstinate.

"Good morning," she answered.

"And what a good morning it is."

Claudia couldn't stop the smiled that tugged at her lips.

"About last night," she started, her insecurities creeping back in. "It was a mistake." Jaden was quiet, so Claudia continued. "I can't be in a relationship with you Jaden, I'm sorry."

"Why are you doing this?"

Claudia shut her eyes and leaned back in her chair.

"I have issues. I can't very well be in a healthy relationship with anyone when I don't know what that entails. I've never been in one before. I wasn't raised in a family that set good examples. Maybe that's why I always settle for losers, but I don't want to hold you back. You deserve a woman who's put together, and unfortunately, that's not me."

"Claudia."

"I'm sorry Jaden, I really am. I'm sincere when I say, I hope you find the woman of your dreams."

"Claudia."

"I have to go."

"Don't hang up." There was a desperate cry in his voice.

Claudia hesitated. "I'm sorry," she said disconnecting the line.

Jaden slammed the cell phone against the wall effectively shattering the smartphone. A wolfish growl seeped from him, and he balled his fists tight causing veins to populate across his forearms. Claudia seemed hell-bent on moving forward in a relationship without him, so why should he even bother? There was no shortage of women in Chicago or elsewhere. He should just move on and let her be.

But no other woman could replace Claudia. She was effectively in his system, cording around his heart like red blood cells. Jaden squeezed his temples. What do you do when the woman you want doesn't want to be with you? His door swung open, and Jonas stepped in taking in the streak against the wall and shattered phone laying on the floor.

Jaden's head snapped up; his mouth set, ready to go off on whoever dared to enter without an invitation. Seeing Jonas, Jaden swallowed the expletive on his tongue.

"Claudia?" Jonas asked.

Jaden agreed without words, shaking his head up and down. Jonas sighed. "Did you tell her?"

Jaden shook his head no.

"Why not? I thought we agreed you would."

Frustration boiled over. "She didn't give me a chance. She just..." Jaden sighed, "Ended our relationship."

"What are you going to do about it?"

Jaden held him with a lethal glare. "I'm not doing a damn thing. She doesn't want to be with me."

"You don't believe that no more than I do."

"She told me she didn't."

"In those exact words?"

Jaden dithered. "She said something to the effect of, I deserved better or some shit. I don't know why she assumes she's not enough for me, it's driving me crazy."

"So, are you giving up?"

"Yeah, I'm done."

Jonas walked towards the window propping his hands behind his back.

"So then, you don't mind if Derek asks her out?" Jonas was referring to one of Jonathon's frat brothers. "He saw her at the wedding and has been asking about her ever since. But because you guys were together, I've been holding him off."

When Jonas turned to Jaden, the savage glare Jaden shot his way was enough to say it all. "What? If you're not going after her, maybe Derek will have better luck, eh?"

"Are you trying to mess with me, Jonas, because I'm not in a playing mood?"

"You're right; it's too soon. I'll wait until you get over her then introduce them."

Jaden grunted. "Derek won't be alive long enough to get the chance," Jaden barked with a venom potent enough that Jonas believed him.

Jonas slid his hands into his pockets. "That's what I thought." He strolled to the door with a whistle on his tongue.

"You said all that to mean what exactly?" Jaden said from behind him.

Jonas glanced over his shoulder. "Simple; you're in love with her. You didn't get a chance to tell her and anybody else won't suffice. Go get her, before someone else does." Jonas strolled out the door, his whistle haunting Jaden.

Chapter Twenty Three

When Claudia swung the door open, she didn't expect to see Desiree standing on the other side.

"What are you doing here?"

"I am welcomed, right?"

Claudia took a step back and pursed her lips. "Of course you are but what are you doing here today?"

"I came to support my little sister's fundraising event."

Claudia's brows rose in surprise. It was official. Today her benefit would go off without a hitch. At least Claudia hoped it would.

"It's a semi-formal event, what are you wearing?"

Desiree pulled her hand from behind her back holding a garment bag.

"You really did come for my event, didn't you?"

"That's what I said."

Claudia traipsed back to her bedroom where Desiree followed her.

"Why? You've never shown any interest in anything I did before."

"Yeah, I'd like to change that."

Claudia turned to her, confused.

"I've been thinking about moving back to Chicago. I miss mom and I," Desiree paused. "I miss the relationship we used to have."

Claudia didn't know what to say.

"I know it seems sudden, but maybe we can start from the beginning."

By the tortured look on Claudia's face, Desiree snickered.

"I don't mean beginning, beginning, I mean, maybe we could get to really know each other. I don't want to live the rest of my life separated from you guys. Life is short, and I hate my job."

This time Claudia snickered. "Okay, but I have to warn you, I'm not much fun."

"Mom told me what happened."

Claudia rolled her eyes. "Of course she did."

"I hope I'm not overstepping my boundaries when I say this Claudia, but I don't want to see you live in regret."

"What are you talking about?"

"If you don't pursue a relationship with Jaden, you'll always wonder what would've happened if you did. How your life would be different."

Claudia sighed. "Don't you think I know that," she snapped. "It's too late anyway, I haven't heard from him since I broke it off."

Desiree peered at her.

"Are you that surprised?" Claudia asked. "It's not like I don't mess up any good thing I have going anyway."

"Sis," Desiree stepped to her laying an affectionate hand on her back to calm Claudia's nerves. "Don't allow our father to have power over you." Claudia whipped her head up. "Don't deny it, I have these same issues myself, and I should probably practice what I preach. But it's easier to give advice than it is to take it."

Claudia put her hands on her hips glaring at Desiree with a scowl.

"What? At least I'm honest. I want to be happy with someone I can live with forever. If I don't get over my abandonment issues, I'll never be able to be in a stable relationship. Let it go, sis, for your sake and Jaden's."

Desiree walked towards the door. "I'm going to get ready so we can leave together, think about what I said."

Claudia teared up. "Damn you, Desiree," she whispered, knowing her sister was right.

"This is beautiful," Desiree cast an eye around Morgan's. "Wow, Claudia, you really pulled this together. I'm so proud of you."

Claudia smiled, but it didn't reach her eyes. "Thanks."

Morgan's was already abuzz when Claudia, Desiree, and Adeline graced the door. From Servers strolling the room with silver trays that held champagne flutes, to the carved crystal angels that sat around the room holding different hors d'oeuvres, Claudia should've been proud of herself. But the tightness in her belly told a different story. She missed Jaden, terribly, and she couldn't get over herself long enough to call and apologize. Claudia thought about it a million times, and it always went something like, *I'm sorry, I'm a dufus, forgive me, I love you.'* But of course, that never happened. Claudia's eyes settled on the place when she spotted Cassie speaking with a handsome middle-aged gentleman.

For a brief moment, Claudia wondered who he was, but she'd be remiss if she said she wasn't a bit happy Jaden wasn't her date. *Don't get too excited, he won't be on the market for long,* that little unforgiving voice whispered.

As if she'd summoned him up, the doors opened, and Jaden strolled in, dressed down in a Brioni tuxedo tailored to his muscled physique just enough to kiss his skin and settle around his sculpted figure. Mmmm, Claudia thought. Desiree leaned to her and whispered.

"You just moaned out loud."

A gasped left Claudia and Desiree snickered.

"That is not funny!" Claudia whispered back.

"Yeah," Desiree said, "it kinda is."

Claudia glared at Desiree.

"Chérie..."

A surge of heat fled across Claudia's skin as she took her vision from Desiree to the gorgeous man in front of her. Jaden's gaze tore through Claudia's flesh making sure to assault every part of her body before making his way back up. Jaden's Adam's apple bobbled then he spoke.

"You look... divine."

Claudia blushed. "Thank you, so do you."

With admiration in his eyes, his lips curved into a wolfish smile. Claudia's nipples hardened, and she didn't know how she would make it out of this event with her panties intact.

"I'd like to introduce you to Samuel Jenkins, Mayor of Chicago." Jaden held his hand out to the man standing next to him that Claudia had yet to take notice of.

"Mayor Jenkins," she reached out to shake his hand. "Thank you for coming. Your attendance is appreciated."

"When I received word of what you were doing for the caregivers of Chicago, I had to come. My mother too had a caregiver before she passed away and I'll do anything to help out where I can."

"Thank you. All donations tonight go to the startup of Caregivers Organization which I plan to open Monday morning."

"Do you have a building in mind?"

"Are you aware of S & M Financial Advisory?"

"Downtown Chicago, I drive by it every morning."

"I co-own that business with Samiyah Manhattan. I was lucky enough to grab another office space in the building so that Caregivers Organization will be our neighbors."

"Excellent," the mayor said. "You're quite a business woman, aren't you?"

"I try," she said with a laugh.

"You're doing a good job. I may be able to send some business your way. We can always use a sound financial advisor or two." Mayor Jenkins turned to Jaden, "I love beautiful, intelligent women, don't you?"

Jaden hadn't taken his gaze off of Claudia. "Indeed, Mr. Mayor, Indeed."

An attendee approached the Mayor pulling him off to the side.

"Excuse me."

Claudia turned to the familiar voice. "Marcus?"

Marcus smiled and held out his hand for a shake. "You remembered my name."

"Yeah, I'm good with those. How did you hear about this event?"

Marcus' smile held steady. "Through the grapevine. I couldn't hear it from you since you never gave me that call to let me know how your car repairs went."

Claudia laughed. Marcus dressed up nicely, considering the last time she saw him, he was in overalls that he'd been working in all day. The guy standing before her was well groomed, dressed in a Tom Ford suit and suede shoes.

"That's probably because Claudia only has time for one man in her life," Jaden challenged with hostility and rancor oozing from his persona.

Marcus glanced from Jaden to Claudia. "And here I thought you weren't looking for a man."

Jaden interrupted Marcus again. "No, she wasn't looking for you." Jaden took a step forward, and Claudia placed her hands on his broad chest successfully halting his advance.

"Hey, look at me," she said staring into his eyes. Jaden dropped his gaze to Claudia and softened immediately. "He heard you."

"Yeah, but did you hear me, chérie?"

Claudia drew in a quick breath. "I couldn't miss it." A small smile danced at the corners of her mouth, and she turned back to Marcus.

"Thanks, Marcus but I'm okay. My cars fine, I've been," she looked back at Jaden, "tied up."

Jaden slowly pulled his gaze away from Claudia back to Marcus. "Step off," he growled.

Marcus made himself scarce, and Claudia smirked up at Jaden.

"Let me find out, you've got a little hood in you.

A devilish smile curved his moist mouth. "We've all got a little hood in us," he winked, "chérie."

A blush fell over Claudia. "Hmmm, I think I like that."

"Do you now?"

"Yes, I do."

"I'll keep that in mind, but first, when did your car have repairs?"

"Oh, I um, it's embarrassing. Unfortunately, ole Betsy broke down on the side of the highway and Marcus is a tow truck driver." She glanced over to him in his Tom Ford suit knowing the ensemble could easily cost a few thousand. "Well at least that's what he was at the time. He towed Betsy to my mechanic's shop."

"And what else?"

Claudia was taken slightly aback by Jaden's questioning.

She folded her arms. "He gave me his number and asked me out, but as you've witnessed, I told him I wasn't looking for a man. Why do you care, Jaden?"

Jaden tensed, and his nostrils flared. He took a step closer further closing the small gap between them.

"You should know, that nothing is going to stop me from having you as my woman." His eyes roamed across the features of her face. "Nothing, chérie. I am as invested in making you understand that we belong together as I am invested in making you scream my name when you come."

A set of chills fled down Claudia's spine, and she shifted her weight from one foot to the other.

"For some reason, you have this idea that you're not good enough for me. But you're mistaken. You're everything I need and more. Do you hear me, Claudia?"

Swallowing hard Claudia responded. "I hear you."

"But do you understand what that means?"

"I've got a feeling you're going to tell me."

Jaden gifted Claudia a half of grin that further set her loins on fire.

"That means, you and I will be together come hell or high water. Nothing would give me more pleasure than to—"

Before Jaden could finish someone glided to stand next to them. Jaden and Claudia looked to their guest, and a smile broke out on Jaden's face. He reached out and slapped hands with his brother.

"Glad you could make it," Jaden said.

"My plane touched down thirty minutes ago. I was already dressed for the occasion." Julian looked to Claudia. "Hey beautiful lady, this is an excellent event you have on your hands. You could use some music or something though. Tell me what you need, I can grace the audience with these vocals if you want. What's your pleasure?"

Julian was just as suave as Jaden but as different as night and day. Where he was constantly on the go because of his international male modeling agency, Julian lived for the attention he received on a regular basis. Having a woman in his life was an afterthought, but he couldn't deny that today he'd taken the opportunity to see Desiree again at Claudia's event. He had no idea Desiree would even be in attendance, but he'd hoped for the best.

"Whatever Claudia needs, I'll be the one making sure she's equipped," Jaden said, "You feel me."

Jaden slid Julian a perilous smile.

"My bad brother, I definitely didn't come to step on your toes," Julian retorted.

"Not if you want to leave with those toes intact."

Julian chuckled the gleam in his eyes making their rounds to Desiree. Desiree stood next to Claudia sipping from a glass of champagne. She'd tried to suppress the smile on her lips, but Julian could see right through her.

"Excuse me," Julian said stepping between Claudia and Jaden to stand in front of Desiree.

"You know I agree with your friend here," a voice off to the side said. Jaden, Claudia, Desiree, and Julian looked to the voice. The middle-aged man eased into their circle and Cassie lingered at his side; the gray strands in his black hair seemingly put together on purpose. The accent he spoke with gave Claudia the impression that he was of Spanish descent but she couldn't be certain. The man held his hand out for a shake.

"Ms. Stevens, besides the cover charge, how do you propose to make money off this event? Is there a live auction slated for later or?"

"No there isn't a live auction, the cover charge and the price per plate is how I plan to gain donations. Unless of course, you'd like to make a generous offer out of the kindness of your heart." Claudia batted her eyes, and the man smirked. "You are?"

"Angelo Garcia," he said introducing himself, "and I'd like to make a proposition."

He'd officially peaked everyone's interest.

"Do you dance, Ms. Stevens?"

Claudia's mouth fell open then closed. "Um, yes, I do."

Angelo chuckled at her hesitation. He cast a look at Jaden who was standing so close to Claudia you'd think they were one person. Looking back at Claudia, Angelo said, "I'd like to challenge you to a duel. You can choose any partner that you wish and so can I. I'll donate one hundred thousand dollars if you can spin the wheels off this crowd better than me." Angelo smiled elated with himself. "What say you?"

"I'll match his one hundred thousand," came a voice standing next to him. Angelo's smiled brightened.

"So will I, came another."

"I'll double it," Mayor Jenkins said, now tuned back into their conversation.

Claudia was on pins and needles. Sure, she could dance, but she had a feeling her moves were slightly different than his and in front of this crowd she was growing stiffer by the minute.

"What do you say, Ms. Stevens? There's currently five hundred thousand dollars on the table. Will you leave it there, or show us what you got?" Angelo turned and pulled Cassie in by her hand. "You're not scared, are you?" He asked.

Claudia's mouth was stuck. There was no way she could beat professional dancers. What kind of game was Angelo playing?

"She accepts," came Jaden's dangerous voice behind her.

Claudia spun around to him. "What?!"

Jaden's eyes swept over her. "Tell him you accept his proposal." He reached out to touch her chin. "You trust me don't you, chérie?"

Claudia turned back to Angelo. "I accept," she said quickly.

Excitement bubbled over in Angelo's face. "Magnifico! Would you like to go first, or shall we?" He pulled Cassie closer, and Claudia took in a deep breath.

"You go first."

"As you wish." Angelo strolled off heading straight for the music center.

Claudia turned back to Jaden. "Oh my God," was all she said.

Jaden pulled his hands from behind his back and grabbed Claudia's hand linking their fingers. "You are an extension of me, remember?"

Claudia swallowed and nodded her head. They turned to watch Angelo and Cassie dance to an upbeat tune. They moved around the floor like they practiced the dance on several occasions and the crowd was engaged; clapping and tapping their feet. Claudia's nerves were a mess, and her stomach curled into knots.

"I don't know if I can do this," she whispered to Jaden.

He held a steady smile on his lips. "You can do anything you want, chérie. You and I together will show them what it's like to move."

Claudia's pulse spiked. Jaden was so sure they could beat the two in a dance off, and his words did shower her with reassurance. Suddenly, she felt like she could do anything with Jaden, and her heart swelled as she watched him watch her.

The dance went on for a full three and a half minutes before it ended. The crowd cheered and clapped. Angelo and Cassie dipped into a bow before strolling in Claudia's direction.

"That was exhilarating!" Angelo said. "It's your turn, are you still in?"

Jaden tightened the hold on Claudia's hand.

"We're in," she said.

A sexy smile fell across Jaden's lips, and they moved to the music center to change the tune. Claudia's heart was racing, and she was trying to keep her wits about herself.

They moved from the music center to the dance floor where Jaden pulled her close. The music began, and a shiver ran through Claudia. It was the same jazz melody he'd played when they danced in the studio months ago. Memories of that time flashed through Claudia's mind, and a smile cruised across her lips.

"Wherever you go, I go," Jaden said repeating what he'd told her previously. "When we touch, our connection should be..."

Claudia finished his sentence, "As if we are one."

A broad smile spread across his lips, and they danced. Their bodies fused together as their hips moved slow and sensual.

"To execute this dance perfectly..."

"Confidence must ooze from your body language," Claudia said again, repeating his instructions from their dance lesson. A sexy rumble bellowed from Jaden as the heat from their magnetism settled between them.

You wouldn't have known Claudia learned to tango this year by the way she shifted in Jaden's arms. Graceful, seductive, and effortless, their chemistry no doubt supercharging her evolution. Claudia imitated Jaden's movements stirring the crowd up as their carnal wine dance began to ruffle the feathers of their attendees. Dipping and swaying, their harmony was so potent their tango was like making love on the dance floor.

Jaden twirled Claudia out, releasing her at once. Claudia back pedaled in her three-inch heels sliding away from him bit by bit. Slowly, she inched her dress up her legs in a tease, as her hips rotated from side to side. Jaden went to reclaim her pulling her flank against his broad chest with ferocity, and Claudia's leg lifted sliding up to his hip in a sensual lock.

Jaden dipped her, and Claudia's head flung back, leaving her neck fully exposed. Jaden's lips trailed from her chin down her throat before he whipped them both back to a stand where they wined and turned in the same order. The cat calls and whistles shouted from the crowd as their tango heated up. When Jaden twirled Claudia again and pulled her back in with rigor, Claudia did something unexpected. Her hand ran down his chest as she slid down his leg into a graceful split. The crowds' cat calls and applause magnified, and Jaden's debonair smile returned as he pulled her effortlessly to stand. They twirled; their limbs coiled around each other so magnificently you would've thought they were one person. Grinding into each other, they soared across the floor in unison like they were born for this. Taking a leap of faith, Claudia held closely to Jaden's ear.

"I miss you," she confessed.

Jaden's eyes twinkled. "Not more than I have missed you, chérie."

"I was thinking," Claudia said as her hands roamed around his chest. "If you were interested in giving us another chance."

Jaden turned Claudia; her backside now tight against his front. "There is not a day that goes by that I haven't imagined us together..." his lips met her shoulder then rested right above her ear. "Forever..."

Claudia's heart rate increased. "Forever?"

Jaden twirled her out and dropped to one knee producing a silver box which he popped instantly. He never took his eyes off of Claudia as a sharp gasp fled her lips. The crowd went crazy as they watched on in anticipation. Cameras rolled and pictures snapped as people held their loved ones' close.

"Chérie, I don't want to spend another moment without you." He reached out to her, "Will you do me the honor and—"

"Yes!" Claudia shouted. And the crowd went wild. A lone tear slid out of Jaden's eye as he placed the ring on Claudia's finger. It was a perfect fit. He placed a kiss on the back of her hand and rose, lifting her in his arms in a twirl. Claudia sank her lips to his lips in a delicious kiss that exploded through them both.

"Alright now, get a room!"

Laughter skittered around. When the couple pulled apart, they turned to see Jonas and Samiyah. Samiyah was dabbing at tears that threatened to fall out of the corners of her eyes. They strolled up to Jaden and Claudia along with Desiree, Julian, Adeline, Angelo, and Cassie.

"Congratulations!" They all yelled.

"Well, there's no way we can top that!" Angelo confirmed.

They all laughed, and Samiyah pointed to Claudia. "Now who's the lucky girl?"

Claudia squealed, elated to be the future Mrs. Jaden Alexander Rose."

The End

Enjoying the Falling for a Rose Series? Grab the next installment which follows Julian Alexander Rose and Desiree Stevens as they venture into a thing called love in, Only If You Dare.

Hey reading family, wow another wild ride with the Rose brother's! I hope you're fanning the flames like I am writing their stories and I hope you've enjoyed this book as much as I enjoyed writing it. If so, take a moment and leave a review on Amazon. Check the next page for other books I have in store and be sure to sign up for my newsletter!

XOXO - Stephanie

More Books by Stephanie Nicole Norris

Contemporary Romance

- Everything I Always Wanted (A Friends to Lovers Romance)
- Safe With Me (Falling for a Rose Book One)
- Enough (Falling for a Rose Book Two)
- Only If You Dare (Falling for a Rose Book Three)

Romantic Suspense Thrillers

- Beautiful Assassin
- Beautiful Assassin 2 Revelations
- Mistaken Identity
- Trouble In Paradise
- Vengeful Intentions (Trouble In Paradise 2)
- For Better and Worse (Trouble In Paradise 3)
- Until My Last Breath (Trouble In Paradise 4)

Christian Romantic Suspense

- Broken
- Reckless Reloaded

Crime Fiction

- Prowl
- Prowl 2
- Hidden (Coming Soon)

Fantasy

- Golden (Rapunzel's F'd Up Fairytale)

Non-Fiction

- <u>Against All Odds (Surviving the Neonatal Intensive Care Unit)</u> *Non-Fiction

About the Author

Stephanie Nicole Norris is an author from Chattanooga Tennessee with a humble beginning. She was raised with six siblings by her mother Jessica Ward. Always being a lover of reading, during Stephanie's teenage years her joy was running to the bookmobile to read stories by R. L. Stine.

After becoming a young adult, her love for romance sparked leaving her captivated by heroes and heroines alike. With a big imagination and a creative heart, Stephanie penned her first novel Trouble In Paradise and self-published it in 2012. Her debut novel turned into a four book series full of romance, drama, and suspense. As a prolific writer, Stephanie's catalog continues to grow. Her books can be found on Amazon dot com. Stephanie is inspired by the likes of Donna Hill, Eric Jerome Dickey, Jackie Collins, and more. She currently resides in Tennessee with her husband and two-year-old son.

https://stephanienicolenorris.com/

Made in the USA
Coppell, TX
23 December 2021

69933924R10144